The Game Room

By William Cladley

EK gewidmet,
weil alle einen Anfang nötig haben.

Contents

Life has a way of settling into a painful routine. The constant tension between possibility and necessity wages an inner war from day to day, and eventually people need to escape. They instinctively search out the small pleasures in life that make the wounds of repetition tolerable and create enough motivation to confront the next day's self-liquidating cycle. All of this is, of course, an illusion, but the more deeply one believes it, the more beautiful it becomes.

At least that is what Randy James told himself as he backed his half-rusted Toyota Tundra up a sharply inclined driveway towards his old three-car garage. The weight of the truck shifted as it rolled up the uneven pavement, causing the vehicle to bob from side to side– undulations which elicited a subtle "fuck" from his lips. He had come this far, and he wasn't about to ruin his prized cargo with an errant pump of the gas pedal, so he cut the engine and hopped into the truck bed to check on the state of his coveted score.

Underneath a tarp was an arcade cabinet– the newest addition to his extensive collection of video game hardware. The cabinet had no real value in and of itself and was, in fact, an amalgam of old particle board from a number of dilapidated arcade machines. The sides were badly worn panels from a *Virtua Fighter* game. The marquee had been removed and replaced with a piece of semi-translucent white plastic that was ever so subtly singed by the heat of the incandescent bulb that rested behind it. The back was unpainted and had spots of an oily, unknown grime that Randy chose to ignore. The only saving grace was that the machine had a brand new OLED monitor and a pair of functional joysticks and buttons. This was not a find, but rather a small luxury, and it cost Randy a significant portion of his wages. Work was infrequent and the wise move would have been to put the $900 he paid for it towards the more pressing necessities of life. But it was 2030, and there were no arcades–let alone arcade cabinets–left in Pennsylvania's Wyoming Valley. This was a relic that he needed to own, made of the stuff that could sustain the grand illusion of escape for another month or two.

After gazing at his find for a bit, Randy dismounted from the truck bed and walked down the long driveway to the street– Prospect Street, Wilkes-Barre, PA. He always found this to be an amusing name for a place that embodied the exact opposite of its title. On the one hand, it looked much like it did in the 1960s. The houses were largely unchanged, save for the rust that engulfed most of the hand railings and window air-conditioners that remained in place regardless of the season. The only elements of the street that revealed the seventy years of social and technological development between its 1960s zenith and its present day reality were the solar panels that powered the street lamps– half of which were broken and flickered on and off as they battled the darkness that threatened to envelop the city. Beyond this one nod to progress, however, Prospect Street was eerily still, with the majority of the houses boarded up and abandoned long ago and clumps of grass fighting their way through the numerous cracks in the pavement.

As dusk settled over the valley, the chill of the approaching winter permeated the air and seemed to intensify the road's desolate aura. Randy peered into the distance. A soft, orange haze emanated from a mining facility perched atop the Game Land Mountains and, blending with the light of the street lamps and of the few houses that remained occupied, created a somber, artificial twilight that consumed the neighborhood. Randy made a call.

"Bro, it's here."

As he reached into his pocket for a cigarette, he heard footsteps coming toward him. They gathered in intensity and mixed with the metallic clang of a chain-link fence, after which a figure approached.

"You got it?" called a young voice from the shadows.

"Yeah, dude. Just like I said. Thanks for helpin'. Cigarette?"

A thin kid walked up to Randy and extended his hand. He had a backpack slung over his right shoulder and wore tattered jogging pants and a plaid, flannel shirt.

"Thanks, dude," he said, grabbing the last of Randy's Marlboros and lighting up, almost in the same motion.

Jared Halacek, known as Jay to the guys left in the neighborhood, was a 21-year-old local tech prodigy who spent his days doing computer repairs for local residents as well as the occasional tech support gig for the Wilkes-Barre city government and local school districts. Although typically withdrawn and socially awkward, he was appreciated for his knowledge and helpfulness to the community. If an old lady's washer broke down and there was no serviceman to call, because no one serviced household goods in Wilkes-Barre anymore, he'd go over and fix it for a reasonable fee. When a school needed to repair a few computers or jerry-rig a server that was 20 years old, he'd do it at a fraction of the cost of calling in the experts. He also wrote bits of code on a freelance basis and had released a few smart phone apps that were fairly popular among the geek community. For a kid that had a shot at getting out of the Wyoming Valley, he seemed to be content to stay and was, in comparison to a lot of people his age and older, thriving in a tough situation.

"You get the top," Randy said, gesturing for Jay to hop into the Tundra.

The two eased the arcade cab onto a hand truck and wheeled it into the garage. Randy flicked on the light switch. The room was bathed in an antiseptic fluorescent light that seemed to belong in a medical clinic rather than a space that was doubling as a game room. Still, it was light, and its severity could not mute the overwhelming comfort that the room offered. It was a meticulously crafted monument to a bygone era. The walls were lined with makeshift shelving, housing thousands of loose and boxed video and computer games. The little wall space that was left over was covered with framed video game posters and magazine cutouts, the bold colors of which were still visible through the thin layers of dust that had collected on and beneath their glass enclosures.

"Fuck," said Jay, gasping and looking around the room, "how much more stuff can you fit in this place?"

"It's almost finished," said Randy, "but there's always something else you can do. The beauty of the game room is in the details, bro. Watch this."

Randy walked to the left side of the room and stood in front of a curious circular shelf housing 4 displays— an old CRT TV, a computer monitor, a mid-2000s era flat-screen and a more modern-looking, off-brand 8K TV that was about a year or two old. The monitors were arranged on the left, right, top and bottom of the shelf, like the ends of a reticle. The space in the middle of the circle had smaller shelves housing video game consoles in order of their

4

release, beginning with the Nintendo Entertainment System and ending with the Playstation 3.

"Let's say I want to play the Genesis," continued Randy, gesturing to a Model One Genesis on the middle-center shelf, "and I know that it would look best on my CRT over here."

"Ok, so what? You just turn it on and play it."

"Nah, you gotta do it with style. Check this out," said Randy, taking hold of a lever and rotating the circular shelf clockwise until his Zenith CRT was at eye level with his couch.

"Shit, dude, that's pretty cool," said Jay. "Did you wire that up yourself?"

"Yeah, got these special made wires from China. Tons of slack. I can rotate this thing three-hundred-sixty degrees."

"I'll give it to you man. That's pretty unique."

"Yup. I got it all hooked up to this switch box. I can just rotate this thing around and go through the whole history of gaming in one night- on the consoles, at least. But now that I got the arcade cab, I can pretty much play every game from 1977 through 2002 if I wanted to."

"Damn," said Jay, "and you actually got time to do that?"

"Don't worry about my schedule, kid. Now let's move this motherfucker into position."

Randy reached down and grabbed the end of the tattered throw rug that covered most of the floor and pulled it back, revealing the cracked concrete beneath it and a few dead stink bugs and spiders that had besieged the game room during the previous summer. He folded up an old card table behind the couch that doubled as a dinner table and moved it to the side. The two then eased the arcade cabinet off of the hand truck and set it down.

"Ok. Now we're gonna have to push," said Randy.

He tilted the machine toward Jay and they attempted to lift and shimmy it into a caddy-corner position on the far right-hand side of the room. It was heavier than it looked and, through his deep breaths of unexpected exertion, Randy noticed the pale white arm of his friend, made visible as the right sleeve of his flannel shirt receded toward his elbow. Jay was seventeen years younger than Randy, but he seemed noticeably weaker, which was especially apparent when looking at the meagerness of his forearm as it strained against the weight of the cabinet. Only the thinnest of muscle sinew flexed forth from the bone, and the milky white of his skin was interrupted by a few flakey red patches that, were it not for the oppressive light of the room, might have remained invisible.

At 38, Randy was by no means a vision of good health, but his frame was filled out, perhaps a bit overweight, and he was still physically capable, owing largely to his part-time gig as a hauler— an independent courier who delivered industrial equipment to various energy stations throughout the region. This arcade machine was heavy, but it really shouldn't have fatigued a 21-year-old kid and yet, as the sweat now poured from Jay's head, beginning at the hairline of his red crew cut and tracing a path downward through the many folds of skin created by his constant grimace, Randy couldn't help but think that he'd asked a bit too much of his friend.

"You okay?" asked Randy.

Jay gulped the stale air of the garage.

"Fine," he said.

"You got the computer?" asked Randy.

"Fuck yeah."

Jay reached into his navy backpack and pulled out a thin, custom-built computer. It was about the size of a small Blu-Ray player, with a top panel made of brushed metal. This aesthetic sensibility and build quality immediately identified it as an "independent design," a designation given to purpose-built computers that were heavily regulated by the FCC and local governments. They were only ever found in universities and corporate research labs, where there was a specific scientific need to build a computer that exceeded the capabilities of a tablet PC, which were the only ones sold to the general public.

"Sweet case," said Randy, reaching for the device.

Jay pulled it back from his grasp. "Where's my $200."

"Jesus, I'll get it."

Randy took off his coat, revealing a Mega Man T-shirt with a few holes on the collar. Sweat had smudged his old wireframe glasses, which he attempted to clean with the back side of his index finger and polish with the lip of his shirt. He adjusted the hair band around his pony tail as he walked to a metal computer desk at the back of the room and removed a wad of cash from the drawer. He peeled off three $50 bills and reached into his pocket for the remaining money, which he paid in $10s.

"You're a prick, kid, but at least you still take cash," said Randy, as he handed over the payment.

Jay smirked. "Open it," he said, gesturing to the arcade cab.

Randy complied, and the second the service door was open, Jay began attaching the power and video cables and securing the PC to the side of the machine's interior with some specially made brackets and screws. All signs of his fatigue had vanished and were replaced with an eager enthusiasm that seemed to grip him every time he was engaged in a technical project.

"Smells like balls in here. Got the SD card?" he asked.

"Here. Careful, though. Don't fuck it up," said Randy.

The SD card was the last of its kind. It was a 256gb card that was about 15 years old, made at a time before storage devices had unique ID chips that would signal to the cloud where and in what device they were installed, get scanned for authorized content and, assuming everything checked out, prompt the user to buy a cloud storage subscription. This card had been specially modified to trick a Windows PC into believing that it was authenticated, thus bypassing all security checks, which typically resulted in unchipped, unauthorized storage being immediately destroyed upon installation into a modern, Internet-connected device. According to the powers that be, private ownership of blank storage fostered terrorism, and unless the storage device was tied to an approved, cloud-based storage provider, it was considered illegal. If an SD card or flash drive was found to have unlicensed entertainment content saved to it, a hefty fine was levied or, if the amount of such content was above a certain, non-specified threshold, the owner could face jail time. A card filled with MAME ROMs of every arcade game ever made, for example, would likely be grounds for incarceration, which is why Randy turned to a professional of sorts to get his new cab up and running.

"Fuck, Windows is asking to authenticate again," said Jay.

"I thought you took care of that already. I'm almost out of Internet for the month," said Randy, his voice cracking with nervousness.

"Nah, it's ok, I'll set up my phone as a hotspot."

Jay reached into his pocket and took out a brand new Samsung smartphone—a kind that was rarely seen outside of a larger metro area. He began typing feverishly with his right thumb, while navigating some menus on the arcade cab with his left hand.

Surprised at how long the process was taking, Randy leaned over his shoulder and tried to get a glance at the screen.

"Look, I didn't register the game room. No one knows about the stuff in here. I haven't paid the device tax on any of it. If they pick up an unauthorized device transmission from in here, I'm fucked," Randy said.

"I got this, man. Don't worry," said Jay, with a sense of confidence spilling over into arrogance. "I masked it to seem like an activation from Senegal. Let Microsoft go hunting there for some tribal motherfucker. You're good. I promise."

Within a few minutes, the new, illegal computer had finished updating, booted into the MAME interface and, glowing forth from the arcade cab, was the entire history of arcade gaming up until 2002. Randy did a cursory scroll through the thousands of titles he had torrented over the years. All seemed to be there and ready to play.

"Awesome, man. Thanks for this. Why don't you play something?" he said, walking to a mini-fridge next to his couch and removing two beers.

"You got the original Street Fighter?"

"Absolutely, but it sucks," said Randy as he tossed a beer to Jay.

Jay cracked it open, took a sip, loaded Street Fighter and began playing. He was visibly amused at playing something so old and so forgotten to gamers of his generation, who spent most of their game time playing on phones and tablets and had, for the most part, only played game consoles as kids. It was therefore a virtual certainty, especially in Wilkes-Barre, that Jay had never seen or touched a real arcade machine before.

"Where the fuck did you find this thing?" Jay asked.

"Guy I know in Scranton who has a warehouse full of old shit. He's pretty handy so he put these pieces together and installed the OLED and the joystick and buttons I wanted. It's probably like the only one of these in the area."

Jay's attention had been diverted back to the game, which was getting progressively harder.

"This game really does suck," he said, throwing his hands up in disgust after a loss and beginning to chug his beer.

"Yeah, let's play Super Street Fighter II," said Randy, scrolling down a massive list of every Street Fighter arcade game variant released from 1987-2001. "It was definitely the best of the classic Street Fighter games."

"You got another beer?" asked Jay.

"Help yourself."

Randy got the game going and motioned to Jay to get on the player two controls. They selected their characters and began fighting. Randy, as always, chose Ken, and began firing off an unstoppable chain of hadukens and dragon punches at Jay's hapless Chun-Li. He glanced down at Jay's hands, which were confused, uncoordinated, and wholly unable to match the pace of play required in Street Fighter. Hands that always gamed on a smartphone didn't have the speed or the accuracy to compete against a seasoned, classic arcade player. Feeling a sense of pity for his friend, he stopped the competition after the fourth match and instructed Jay to play against the computer. He set the game to 3 in the softdip settings and began methodically instructing his friend on the finer points of the game: the difference between quarter-circle/half-circle characters and charge characters, the importance of spacing, and strategies for drawing opponents into basic combo attacks. As they progressed through the lesson, Jay slowly dropped the veneer of arrogant techno-certitude and began asking questions and taking instruction like a kid brother attempting to learn the secrets of a heretofore unknown realm of adult life. When they switched back to competitive play, he got better, began to internalize the character move-sets and played a more aggressive, skillful game.

Throughout this Street Fighter master class of sorts, Randy couldn't help but think to himself that *this* was why the game room needed to exist—to preserve an experience that was ubiquitous in the 90s, but all but forgotten in the chilly industrial hinterlands of 2030s Northeastern Pennsylvania. This was gaming without subscription fees, without paid DLC, without the networked panopticon that made players agree to share their in-game data with unnamed third parties performing "demographic research and decision path analysis." It was two guys, in front of a machine, absorbed in the refined control mechanics and colorful sprites of a lost generation of gaming.

As the competition between the two friends continued at a heated pace, a soft but persistent chime emanated from Jay's phone.

"Let me just finish kicking your ass before you get that, bro," said Randy.

"Fuck it, one more round."

The chime continued.

"Come on, man, that thing's been going for a while now, see who it is or just put it on silent."

"Probably just my girl, Blake," said Jay.

The phone finally stopped and the two continued their battle, now somewhat drunk as they polished off their fourth beers. They had entered the proverbial "zone." Players old enough to remember playing games in actual arcades will attest to the existence of the zone—a psychological space where the connection between the player and arcade machine became more intimate, where the best players became absorbed in the lights and sounds of a game and their reactions became ever more accurate. It was a pleasurable human-machine interaction that did not exist in the world of 2030 America and could only be simulated—with the aid of free time and alcohol—by those dwindling numbers of people who still owned physical games. The stronger the buzz, the more the outside world faded away in favor of a comforting nostalgia for the good old days of gaming.

As the competition continued, Randy heard a soft whirring sound that was becoming increasingly distracting. He glanced around the room in between matches with increasing paranoia until he finally paused the game.

"You hear that?"

"Hear what?" growled Jay.

"That fucking buzzing sound. Is that the computer?"

"Computers don't buzz anymore. What are you? 50?"

"Come on, I know you hear that," said Randy.

He began pacing around the room, putting his ear up to the various electronic devices and consoles on his shelves in an attempt to ascertain the source of a noise that was instinctively worrying to a vintage electronics collector.

As Randy was inspecting his large, circular display shelf, Jay shouted, "Fuck! We're getting patrolled!"

"What?"

"Fuck man, a patrol drone is coming!" shouted Jay.

"Patrol drones? They never come this far into the city."

"I've got a tracker app, bro. It's out there. I'm fucking dead serious."

"Unbelievable!" said Randy, as he flicked off the master power switch to the game room and disconnected the battery back-up system from his computer.

"Check this out," said Jay, holding up his phone to Randy from a prone position on the floor, "it says this is one of those military grade drones. The FL-Z10-Search and Compliance. Some shit must be going down around here."

Randy took the phone and squinted as he attempted to bring the small red dot circling his house into focus. "Fuck, you really think that's what we're hearing? I didn't think those things existed."

"According to this tracker app they do, and the fucker is out there now," whispered Jay in response.

While the use of drones had become a fairly standard practice in American society quite a while ago, there were rumors floating around that a new breed had come into service in some police precincts over the past few years. Unlike the small delivery drones and police safety patrol drones that were the size of a house cat and almost whisper quiet, these so-called search and compliance drones were supposed to be the size of three or four motorcycles lined up side by side, and were equipped with multiple search lights, electronic surveillance arrays, and rifles to eliminate criminal threats. They also had the reputation of being noisy, possessing what was said to be the acoustic signature of a weed-wacker locked in a car trunk. Very few people had seen them, of course, and reports of their existence were typically confined to the dark web and were hard to substantiate. Those who believed in their existence would defend the overall lack of evidence about them with the sardonic observation that, if you did see one, you wouldn't be in a position to report your findings.

The two lay silent and motionless on the floor of the game room and listened for further signs of the drone's patrol. The whirring that spooked Randy earlier was now very faint, but the red dot on Jay's phone was still circling around Prospect Street. They watched its pattern move in a slow, counter-clockwise direction, but the late autumn breeze outside made it hard to distinguish any mechanical sounds from the rustling leaves and the soft hiss of wind penetrating the drafty walls of the garage.

After about 10 minutes, Jay got up and crept over to one of the garage doors and pressed his ear against it. Within seconds of doing so, there was a powerful snarl of air that seemed to rush toward the opposite wall of the room. Jay dropped down and pressed his thin body parallel to the garage door, as Randy, unable to move fast enough from the center of the room, remained on the floor in utter helplessness. A searchlight blasted through the window above the metal computer desk and scanned the room. Neither friend was completely hidden from its glow. The motors and propellers then spun up and they could hear the drone swing around to the front of the garage, at which point it again cast its searchlight into the room, although this time it had a pale, red hue and pulsated as it moved in a slow pattern from left to right. The light then cut off and it sounded as if the drone had flown off in the opposite direction.

Randy and Jay remained on the floor, as if anchored in the concrete, and listened intently. Neither of them wanted to risk moving too soon, and probably couldn't move at all even if they had wanted to, as they were both paralyzed with fear and uncertainty. The shaking of their bodies was made evident by the trembling of their deeply drawn breaths, which produced an audible quiver in the room and created the illusion of a phantom heartbeat, pounding in syncopation to their own.

Jay eventually took the risk of speaking.

"What do we do, bro? You think we should get out of here?"

"Are you fucking nuts?" said Randy. "If anything's out there—more drones, police, anything—we're totally fucked."

"But what if that thing comes back for us?"

"Then it comes back for us. Nothing we can do now. We're way safer in here than driving around the streets at this point."

"I don't know, dude," said Jay, "Those FL-Z10s could fucking scorch this place if they wanted to. I read they have this sick weapons array that can fuckin' ventilate a building."

"Don't you know anything, kid?" said Randy, forcing aggression through a whisper. "There are rules around here. Keep your head down. Stay indoors. Pay your bills online. And avoid the FUCKING cops! I don't see any cops in here, but who the fuck knows what's going on out there. So just lay the fuck on the floor and don't act like a fucking pussy."

"Fine. But what're we going to do?"

"We wait."

"Fuck you been?" shouted a drill site foreman as Randy parked his Tundra in the contractor loading area of Mega Drill 7, a massive drill site 20 miles outside of Wilkes-Barre.

"Sorry, got my hauls confused," replied Randy, his eyes still adjusting to the brightness of the midday sun.

"Didn't you see the fuckin' notification on the app?" said the foreman.

"I had a long night. Sorry."

"Whatever… Look, you and some guys got the waste haul today. Whole fuckin thing's been delayed on account ah you. The processing depot needs to take delivery of this shit all at once, so thanks for wasting everyone's time. You're lucky if you get half of the pay for this job, asshole."

"Sorry, man. I haven't had a tardy in like 2 years," said Randy.

"Yeah, well, there's a million losers like you who can make it here on time to haul shit," said the foreman, gesturing to Randy to follow him to the far side of the loading area. "My guys are gonna secure two drill rods to your truck. You gotta drop'em off at Bay 8 of the processing depot. In the meantime, help load up the liquid waste haul onto those trucks. They're going to follow you to the depot, so make sure you use your flashers and your warning lights. No stopping. The less that shit shifts around, the better."

Randy was no stranger to the blunt authoritarianism that accompanied work in the Marcellus Shale Formation, an underground rock layer that stretches from central New York State, through Pennsylvania and West Virginia, and finds its most southerly point in Tennessee. Maryland, Ohio and New Jersey rest on its periphery and share a small fraction of its mineral deposits. During the industrial revolution in the United States, the region produced the iron, coal and anthracite that fueled the growth of the young nation and helped create the industrial foundation which made the post-World War II and high-tech boom periods possible. As time passed, however, and manufacturing withered, factory jobs were sent overseas and most of the region was considered to be part of the so-called Rust Belt–a stretch of Northern U.S. cities which time and opportunity had left behind.

This designation, however, was short-lived. In the mid-1990s, energy companies realized that Marcellus Shale was a vast, untapped reservoir of natural gas and oil that could be extracted through a variety of new technologies, including hydraulic fracturing–the process of drilling deep wells into rock layers and injecting them with a stream of corrosive fluid that would release previously unreachable resources. People protested the expansion of the practice in the mid-to-late 2000s, but by 2018 the proponents of hydraulic fracturing had drowned out the nay-sayers. The promise of jobs, energy independence, and a cultural and economic renaissance had gripped the hearts and minds of the people who lived above the shale. By 2020, the big money did begin to flow and everyone got a taste of the profits. The molecules that were once trapped in a seemingly impenetrable geological tomb had created a new energy boom that revitalized the region. By 2030, no one spoke of "resource extraction" or "fracking," but rather of an "Energy Corridor" that would make the United States an unquestioned leader in the export of natural gas, oil, and energy mining technologies.

The Corridor began in small, distant towns tucked away in the hills of Pennsylvania, New York, and Ohio, where the first drills were installed, but as the drilling technology advanced and the demand for energy grew, these wells expanded to cover the majority of the region and encroached upon even the most densely populated cities, to the point that they became an accepted, almost invisible part of the landscape. The people who initially protested the expansion relocated, and those who remained grew accustomed to the rhythmic pulses of the drills and the liquid torrents that danced beneath their feet.

Two energy companies came to dominate business in the shale fields– Independence Energy, Inc. and Geo Services Corporation. Hundreds of smaller companies relocated to the region to build the economies of scale necessary to make the shale fields globally competitive. Isolated drill sites with a drill tower, a trailer and a porta-potty became integrated into a network of high tech infrastructure as rich and polymorphous as the deposits it was designed to extract–a network serviced by miles of private roads, railways, and office buildings that stood in the once isolated valleys. Luxury accommodations were built in the last green patches of land left in the Corridor and were given to the technicians and executives who managed the operations of the fields and who were often rotated between the Energy Corridor and similar sites in Texas and Western Canada. What made the Corridor unique was that, in addition to fracking, its businesses began to include the refurbishment and reactivation of nuclear power plants, the construction of so-called "clean coal" power plants, and the creation of a vast storage and disposal network for liquid fracking waste produced in the U.S. and abroad.

The Wyoming Valley of Northeast Pennsylvania, and the city of Wilkes-Barre in particular, found itself right on the edge of this high tech leviathan—close enough for its residents to find work in the glowing fields west of the Susquehanna River, but far enough away not to live next to a mega drill. The citizens of Wilkes-Barre were even included in regional profit-sharing agreements with Independence Energy and Geo Services Corp. that paid them $1000-$2000 per month if they owned property in the city. The downside, however, to the geological coincidence that placed the Marcellus Shale Formation just to the west, was that the unrelenting technological development that had transformed forgotten mining towns into gleaming monuments of industrial progress had never expanded into the municipality itself. Wilkes-Barre managed to exist in the region, but was not fully integrated into the system. It had a small, developed downtown shopping district that—from the right vantage point—gave the impression of belonging to a large, affluent metro area, but was in actuality a flashing anomaly of development in an expanse of post-industrial decay. It was as if an invisible barrier had been erected between the city and progress itself, which seemed to call out from the horizon—the glow of the future existing just beyond the shadows of the past.

Randy was thus a time traveler, driving from the gloomy recesses of American history into the glistening, metallic sea of progress to work in the high-tech fracking economy. It was a well-paid, predictable gig, at least until today. This was the first time he had ever been asked to do a hazardous waste haul, and he felt unprepared for such a delicate process. His previous waste hauls had been driving geological samples from one site to another, but he had never worked with actual, spent drilling fluid before. A worker handed him gloves and an eye guard and he began wheeling canisters from a hanger to the lift gate of a tractor trailer. There was a palpable tension to the operation, as the workers in the truck slid the canisters into neat rows and tied down each row with security cable. The cargo was heavier than Randy anticipated and he strained more and more as the day went on, which caused an unusual pain to grow in his chest. At first, he feared that he might be experiencing the symptoms of a heart attack, but his rudimentary knowledge of human anatomy told him that cardiac chest pain is often a crushing sensation in the center of the chest, whereas his pain felt like an expanding ball of tension under his lower-right sternum. He tried to take little breaks from his work to stretch himself out, but the indignant screams of the foreman forced him back into action, never giving him the proper time to loosen whatever compression of bone or tissue was causing his pain.

As his body began to fatigue and his attention was drawn away from his job and toward this odd sensation, he failed to realize that one of the canisters did not have a perfectly secured lid. As he and a fellow worker positioned it on the lift gate and Randy, exhausted and gasping for breath, pulled the hand truck back prematurely, it tipped over, at which point its lid burst off and a huge splash of bright, milky yellow fluid made contact with Randy and his partner.

"Fuuuuuuuuck!" the man shouted as he looked down at his half-soaked uniform.

"Oh shit, I'm so sorry," said Randy, staring at the liquid stain on his own sweater and jacket.

"Oh my god! Oh my god! What the fuck were you thinking?!" said the man in what was now a hoarse scream.

The foreman rushed over to inspect the situation.

"Which one ah you assholes blew your load?" he asked with a toxic laugh. "Abdul, go change and take a half hour to yourself. This asshole hauler's gotta drive home with this shit on him."

"I am really sorry. But, come on, can't I just clean up as well?" asked Randy.

The foreman reached for the walkie-talkie on his shoulder.

"Hazmat to bay 7," he said, smiling and looking down at the yellow stain on Randy's clothes. "Yeah, fuckface, I do mind. Those rods gotta be in Wilkes-Barre in an hour. You were late and you fucked up once you got here. Why the fuck should I care what you got on you? You're lucky I don't file a complaint. Now get the fuck outta here. And you better pray no one lights a cigarette between now and the time you pull into that depot."

Randy went back to his truck and saw that the two rods had been secured in position. They looked like huge, rusty nails that were pulled from a floorboard and they were still wet with what seemed to be the same liquid that had spilled on him. The drive back to town seemed longer than usual, even though the access highway was completely empty and he was traveling at a brisk 85 mph. He was forced to keep the windows open, as the stench in the car was unbearable—a combination of tar and gasoline that got worse as time went on.

Unable to continue breathing in the fumes emanating from his clothes, Randy signaled to the convoy of trucks behind him to drive on and pulled off onto a highway rest area just before the entrance to Wilkes-Barre. He jumped out of the car and, seeing that the parking lot was empty, stripped down to his underwear and collapsed onto the pavement, breathing in the cool air of the early evening and clutching the lower right side of his chest. While on the ground, he began the full routine of stretches and contortions that he couldn't get through at the drill site, his bones and ligaments shifting with the satisfying clicks of a cracked knuckle.

His pain was now subsiding, and he went back to his truck and grabbed his soaked ball of clothes from the front seat. There was no way to dry them completely, as it was too dangerous to expose them to the heat of his radiator. The only thing he could do was wave and shake them in the air, hoping that the thick, flammable liquid deposits would evaporate to the point that he could get dressed and make his delivery. His work was deliberate—first the sweater, then his jacket, and finally his pants. The daylight faded as he tried to jostle the last bit of liquid from his clothing, and he took notice of the uneven illumination of Wilkes-Barre, which stood in front of him like the shadowy, electric cloud of an approaching storm. He realized that he was within the boarder—right on that invisible line separating the Corridor from the ghostly cities it had yet to consume.

Randy was the quintessential inhabitant of this borderland. Having been born in 1992, he grew up with memories of the Rust Belt, experienced the exuberance of the Internet boom, the sting of the Great Recession, the promise of shale and the reality that it ultimately created. He was the last of the millennials, which meant that he was too young to have shared in their earlier advantages and to have participated meaningfully in their culture. Depending on one's point of reference, he may easily have been considered one of the first members of Generation Z, but was, for all practical purposes, too old to be accepted into their ranks. He had enough education to be insightful, but too little to be fully employable in the new technological order that existed less than five miles from his home. Circumstances saved him from poverty, but anchored him in stagnation, allowing him to be insulated from the extreme economic brutalities of the era, while ensnaring him in a mild but consistent state of personal desperation. He had no full time job, no girlfriend, no lasting social connections, and found himself at an intersection of life where the question of one's future is influenced by opportunity and regret in equal measure.

He was born into a typical northern Pennsylvania family. His father was one of the last stably employed factory workers in the city and his mother was a teacher at a local elementary school. His earliest memories were happy, at least from a distance of three decades—a distance that begins to substitute the intricacies of actual experience with a broad, comforting nostalgia. He lived with his parents on Prospect Street, in the same house in which his father had lived as a child. His grandfather built it in the 1940s near the end of the region's first boom period, and the family could never muster the resources or inclination to move. Life was just too comfortable. There were new cars in the driveway, presents under the Christmas tree, and a predictable vacation to Vermont or Cape Cod every year. In 1992, these circumstances were very much rooted in the post-World War II social order that promised security and predictability in exchange for routine and consistency. The rhythms and expectations of the life into which Randy was born were such unquestioned realities of American society that people couldn't perceive or interpret their decline.

For the James family, however, the decline began when Randy was 9 years old. Two months after United Flight 93 crashed in Shanksville, Pennsylvania during the September 11th terrorist attacks, Randy's father lost his factory job when a new facility was opened in Tennessee and he refused to relocate.

Following several months of drinking and job searching, he left the family "in pursuit of work," as he put it, but had instead moved across town to live with a woman he met online. Though devastated, Randy's mother relied on her firm entrenchment within the protestant work ethic to earn a living and make her way through a simple divorce proceeding that allowed her to keep the house and give Randy as normal a childhood as possible—one filled with the typical obligations of school, homework, clubs and healthy doses of video games. He saw his father infrequently, but the time they did spend together was rather light-hearted and not overly inflected with regret or resentment. They would take in the occasional sci-fi film or catch a minor league baseball game, and their conversations never probed the depths of the past or focused on the possibilities of the future. They seemed content to forge a relationship of sustainable, if superficial, conversation that allowed them to exist in the same room as father and son as long as they both had something to divert the bulk of their attention.

Randy graduated high school in 2010 and attended Bloomsburg University in the fall, a reasonably priced college forty miles south of Wilkes-Barre that he attended debt-free thanks to the diligent savings that his mother had managed to scrape together. It was a modest institution made up of rows of clean, modern brick buildings tucked into the northeast end of one of the many non-descript cities along Route 80, the highway that spans the whole of the state and terminates in Youngstown, Ohio. It was a good place for a directionless student to wait out the global economic collapse of 2008 and emerge into what many had hoped would be a fully recovered economy. Randy bounced around from major to major—from Computer Science to English to

Education, before settling on Communications. It was a clichéd, hopeless major, but it was one in which Randy excelled and, since he had no college debt, one that he believed he could use to jump into a Master's degree program in a related field after graduation.

As unimpressive and poorly researched as his future plans may have been, they ceased to be a concern when, in the Spring of his junior year, his mother died of a brain aneurysm in the faculty bathroom of her elementary school. Her colleagues reported that she was complaining of nausea during a lunch break and had excused herself. When she was fifteen minutes late for the start of her class, the school principal went into the restroom and found her collapsed and drooling, her faced pressed into the drainage grate in the center of the floor. Randy's father could not be reached, so it was up to Randy to drive home, identify the body, and begin making funeral arrangements. His father eventually showed up and helped plan the modest services, after which he moved back into the house with Randy and spent the summer in a long silence interrupted only by the crack of opening beer cans and the hum of microwave dinners. It was during this time that Randy moved many of his things into the garage that would later become his game room.

When he returned to Bloomsburg in the fall for his senior year, he was unfocused and detached from his career planning and the graduate school application process. He finished his coursework, skipped graduation, and began working at a Best Buy. The plan was to stay there for about six months and save money for grad school, but time went on and six months became a year.

The job didn't pay much, but it had some benefits. He enjoyed a nice employee discount, which allowed him to fill out his video game collection, and he was eventually promoted from being a cashier to working in the HDTV section, which meant less repetition and more of an opportunity to demo technology to customers. While this work was, in the end, as equally mindless as upselling extended warranties on DVDs at a checkout counter, he felt the illusion of autonomy as he marched around the TV section and explained the intricate differences between HDMI cables to customers who were all too willing to part with their money. It was a low-paid, insecure, but ultimately predictable and low-stress professional inertia that was very comfortable to inhabit.

One night, after returning home from work, he discovered his father dead in his armchair from a self-inflicted gunshot wound. He was sitting hunched over to his right side, dripping blood onto the floor. His face was disfigured from the bullet entry, with his cheeks blown apart and his chin dislodged and hanging from his face. His eyes bulged gently from his skull and behind him was a diffuse spray of blood, tissue and bone fragment. As Randy inspected the room in a state of numbed silence, he noticed a folded piece of paper on his father's snack table next to a can of beer and a half-eaten sandwich. It was short and painful, at once the most heartfelt and honest sentiment his father had ever communicated to him, but also the bluntest and most incomplete.

"Dearest Randall, I fucked up everything. You and Mom deserved more. I know you can't forgive me. I love you. I'm sorry."

Each short sentence deserved an explanation. Each could have formed a bond between father and son or at least have been the start of a mended, semi-authentic relationship. Instead, they were the unexplained riddles with which Randy was abandoned and which he had a lifetime to contemplate. He was in the room with the bleeding corpse of a man who had apparently loved him, but who had never bothered to express the emotion for fifteen years. He suppressed his confusion, anger and sense of abandonment in favor of the more certain and immediate feelings of shock and disbelief, which ultimately allowed him to overcome this second, more visceral trauma.

With his father's death, he inherited the house, which had been paid off long ago by his grandfather. He also became the beneficiary of his mother's life insurance policy, which was an annuity that paid $30,000 a year for the foreseeable future. His father had about $5,000 in the bank at the time of his death, which Randy used to pay for a simple cremation. There were no family members left to contact and no funeral. He simply placed his father's ashes in the basement next to some of his grandfather's old tools.

The crippling loneliness and isolation in the immediate aftermath of his father's suicide gave way to a detached curiosity and reflectiveness. He began to acknowledge a strange, powerful sense of freedom that intermingled with the sadness of the empty house. It was a type of freedom that no one can experience unless they are truly alone in the world, with no spouses or children to provide domestic continuity in the absence of parents. He became obsessed with the limitless possibilities of the future and increasingly unburdened by the traumas of the past—and his modicum of financial security made these possibilities more than mere fantasies. At 22, he was a homeowner with a guaranteed income. He could sell the house and move anywhere. He could quit his job, work part-time, and go to school. It was a freedom that cut through the deafening stillness of his day-to-day life and helped him cope with his new existence in a world in which no one loved him, no one could help him, and in which very few people even knew him.

The dangerous thing about freedom and youth, however, is that both seem eternal and there is no pressing need to come to terms with this illusion. Randy quit his job at the Best Buy and began working in an independent vinyl record shop during the height of the retro culture boom, but he never went back to college. He researched the best cities in the country for single professionals, but never moved. Each passing week allowed him to use his disposable income to pursue new and different hobbies, which became surrogate journeys for the exploration of life that he was deferring. As culture became an insular, networked pursuit within social media and recognition and purpose were measured in likes and retweets, there became less pressure to pursue the life he thought he wanted and every opportunity to enjoy a self-curated, virtual existence within the comfortable and infinitely pleasurable niches of pop, retro, and consumer culture.

By 2020, six years had passed since his father's death and his curious personal emancipation. He was living in the same circumstances and had made very little progress in the so-called real world, although he was known online as a discerning collector of video games and vintage electronics and enjoyed modest popularity in the online communities dedicated to these pursuits. A year later, a waste processing and storage facility opened on the outskirts of Wilkes-Barre and he was enrolled in the city-wide resident compensation plan, which paid him $1,000 per month based on the location, value, and possible environmental impact on his property—more guaranteed income that made exiting his cocoon of retro culture less appealing. Because of this, he was oblivious to the rapid decline that began to happen around him. Businesses in the city not directly connected to the Corridor started to leave, neighborhoods emptied as people sought opportunities deeper within the Marcellus Shale fields, and crime and enhanced policing became commonplace in the streets. He lived in the same city in which he was born, but began to inhabit a different world.

When traveling through the shale fields, Randy would often take a certain solace at being a small part of a larger, transformative technological change that, while certainly not making his own life better in any measurable way, had the potential to revolutionize the country. Tonight, however, it was clear that working in the Corridor could also have a dark side. He felt a deep sense of revulsion as he pulled his still damp clothes over his body and felt the sting of benzene hit his nostrils. His headlights revealed a large, red rash on the side of his stomach where the liquid had soaked through his sweater, and his hands were covered in a thin, white film that refused to peel off, even as he scraped it with his house keys. Once convinced that he could do no more to rid himself of the stench of the Corridor, he made his delivery, drove home, and fell asleep under a hot shower.

The next day, Randy was called out for an early delivery on Highway 7B, which ran from East to West across the main shale plane, between the old Highway 6 and Interstate 80. It was an immaculate four lane road suspended above the landscape by thick steal pillars and provided access to 700 drilling sites. Even with a max speed limit of 100 mph, it took a good two-and-a-half hours of nonstop driving to get from Wilks-Barre to Oil City, the final exit about fifty miles from the Ohio border. The highway offered huge shoulders that functioned as rest areas for drivers who were tasked with traversing the region two or three times in a given day, and had metal picnic tables and a variety of top-of-the-line vending machines that could prepare hot-meals in under ten minutes.

Randy pulled off into one of these rest areas on the eastbound side of the highway, after running his shipment of 200 hundred tablets to a drill site in the Asylum oil fields. He went over to an unoccupied vending machine and ordered his favorite dish—fresh roast beef with jalapeno peppers and artisanal mayonnaise. $16.50. Well worth it.

As it was 1:00pm and most picnic tables were filled with haulers enjoying their lunches, he staked out a spot on the railing at the edge of the highway- a huge silver tube with inset LED lighting and spots for drivers to eat and take in the view. The tube rose to just above chest height, slightly compromising the sight-line to the valley below, but still offering a solid panorama of the mountain tops and mega drills, which created the impression of a cityscape on the near horizon. Drilling was constant throughout the day, and from the suspended highway one could hear each drill site activate and deactivate in an orchestra of faint hums and metallic pulsation. Occasionally, if the conditions were clear and the sun was shining, one could also see streams of red liquid burst through the side of a mountain or hilltop and cascade downward towards the valley. As Randy peered off into the distance and enjoyed his roast beef sandwich and a bottle of Pellegrino, he felt his smartphone vibrate. He checked it to find a text message from Jay.

"Anything from the other night?"

"Nope. Nothing. No cops. Passed a security check on 7B this morning."

He savored the last few bites of his lunch.

"Shit. What was it then?" replied Jay

"No clue. If it was something, we'd know by now."

Randy hopped back into his truck and proceeded east to get back to Wilkes-Barre. It was unusual to have a run-in with a police patrol drone and not deal with any kind of repercussions. Even when you went through a routine security scan with a drone at some of the larger drill sites, the interaction was recorded on the Hauler Drive App and you could see a history of all of your checkpoints and their results. If you were stopped for speeding in town or were scanned into a sporting event by a drone, you would receive an email detailing the interaction. The drone that scanned the game room the other night, if it was one of the newer Search and Compliance types that Jay thought it was, would have certainly created a log that was registered somewhere—and if the police had a reason to use that kind of drone to investigate someone, it was unthinkable that there would not be an immediate follow-up action. And yet, neither Randy or Jay heard anything or were restricted in any way from doing their jobs, both of which required daily security checks and clearances. Jay had even done some tech support for the city, which had the most stringent security protocols, and he was not flagged or questioned. It seemed as if their encounter was either a case of mistaken identity or that the drone really wasn't an FL-Z10. Either way, Randy thought it best not to linger on the experience and simply view it as an aberration or a bad dream. Paranoia was only psychologically meaningful in an age when privacy and relative self-determination were possible. Residents of the Corridor, however, had become accustomed to the reality that they were being watched all of the time and that, if they were truly guilty of an infraction, it would come to the surface sooner or later. It seemed that the dual activation attempts on an unregistered, independent design PC were too minor to be considered prosecutable offenses and that, even if they had been recorded, they were not worthy of sending a cutting edge drone to investigate.

As Randy found himself in a line of trucks waiting to go through a security scan, he checked his phone again. Jay had sent another text.

"Can me and Blake come over to the game room to chill?" he asked.

"Sure. Is Blake that girl you were mentioning?"

"Yeah. They don't let me into the dorms at her school, so we can't really hang out anywhere else."

"See you later then," said Randy.

He went through the checkpoint without issue and proceeded through the streets of Eastern Wilkes-Barre to get home. It wasn't often that he had company beyond Jay and the occasional visits by some other local gaming enthusiasts, but he assumed that Jay's use of the word "chill" was code for "drink", so he stopped off at a local liquor store on his way home. He chose one that still accepted legacy debit cards and cash, rather than the now ubiquitous swipe-to-pay stores that were the standard means of shopping for 95% of people in the region. If you swiped too frequently for alcohol or junk food, you'd be besieged with numerous emails and texts reminding you of the dangers of excessive alcohol and fat consumption. If you chose to ignore these warnings for too long, it would result in a slight increase in your health insurance premiums.

The cash stores, however, had the reputation of being dangerous places, so most people avoided them. In actuality, they were just rundown mom and pop operations—among the last left anywhere—that served as a refuge for the desperate alcoholics who were still on the streets. Randy's favorite was a corner store with a white awning that read "Spirits/Food/Check Cashing" in thick red letters, but seemed not to have an actual name. He went in and grabbed two six packs of Yuengling and two pre-made pizzas that were resting under a warming light. It was not exactly the ideal meal to serve to guests, but it was the best that he could do.

When he arrived home, Jay and Blake were waiting outside of the garage, huddled together, fighting the cold, and smoking cigarettes. Randy got out and handed the pizza and beer to Jay, who struggled to balance the six packs on top of the pizza boxes. As he opened the garage door and turned on the lights to the game room, it occurred to him that he had never shown the room to a woman before and, though he was eighteen years older than Jay's girlfriend and resigned to his quasi-involuntary bachelorhood, he felt nervous in anticipation of her reaction. The shelves of hardware, the revolving wheel of monitors, the stacks of vintage games, and now the arcade machine—all of this was a monument to his youth and the culture that he loved, but he was cognizant of the fact that only he and a select few other enthusiasts would see it as such. Half-embarrassed, he gestured for his guests to come in.

"Fucking incredible, right?" said Jay, putting his arm around his girlfriend as she took in the room.

"Oh my god," she said with genuine surprise, "this is even cooler than you said."

While Jay had mentioned to Randy a few times that he had a girlfriend, he had never produced a picture or text message from her to prove her existence. This is not to say that Randy doubted his friend's ability to be with a girl, but he was surprised that they were dating, as it was his understanding that younger people didn't date in the traditional way, but rather organized their relationships via the Internet or via specialized dating apps that allowed them to "hook-up" when they had the time. There were no longer concepts such as "a couple" or "Facebook official," at least not in the Corridor, where young people, if they hadn't moved away by the time they were done with college, spent most of their days working various jobs and did not reliably have the free time to devote to traditional dating. Thanks to the *Energy Corridor Flexibility and Productivity Initiative*, most people did not even have a traditional weekend at their disposal, as the law restructured the work week in such a way that people worked seven days a week and could then schedule the 32 hours of free time that were typically available in a weekend at various points throughout a seven-day sequence, or save them and put them towards a block of vacation time. Apps and services subsequently sprung up that allowed young people who lived and worked within the context of this and other productivity initiatives across the country to coordinate their free hours and meet up with each other—for everything from marital free time, to steady hook-ups, to random casual encounters. In a comically cruel twist of fate, Randy, being one of the few people left in the region with some consistent free time, found that he would be downvoted in the casual encounters section of these apps because having too many available hours was seen as a less desirable trait. In any event, it was refreshing to see that his friend was engaged in an old school relationship.

Blake appeared to be a reasonable match for Jay. She was twenty years old, a junior at Scranton University, and, like him, seemed to have good prospects for landing a job outside of the city. They even had an amusingly similar fashion sense, as her large gray sweatpants, over-sized, Asian-style parka, and tattered long-sleeved camisole was a perfect match for his familiar sweatpants and plaid look. Her skin was paler than Jay's and she wore her dirty blond hair tied in a tight pony tail that almost erased the boundary between her forehead and hair. The plainness of her appearance was disrupted only by her large, green eyes that revealed a subtle sadness and vulnerability from beneath the veneer of youth. Her chin and severely chapped lips seemed constantly to be on the verge of a quiver, but her lighthearted banter and innocent curiosity managed to suppress whatever deeper impulse was struggling to emerge.

"So how the fuck did you get all of this *stuff?*" she said, grabbing a slice of pizza and a beer and sitting down, cross-legged, at the old card table in the center of the room.

"Just collected it over the years. It's my hobby and since no one else is doing it these days, I just decided to go for it, I guess," said Randy, somewhat suspicious at her interest in the room.

"This guy's the fucking boss when it comes to this stuff," said Jay, after downing his second beer.

They finished their meal of rough and ready pizza and had made their way into the second six pack of Yuengling, with Jay and Randy polishing off their beers in quick succession and Blake nursing her second one and listening intently to Jay recount the events of the "drone strike," as he called it, and how he was close to landing a full time position with the city's data analysis contractor. The conversation then turned back to the game room itself, how long it took to build, how much it cost to amass the collection, and what Randy planned to do with it in the future. Jay even insisted that they take a tour, with Randy offering brief explanations of the games and systems that dotted the walls and why they were significant. They ended the history lesson at the new arcade machine, which Jay turned on to show off his handy work.

"See," he said, scrolling quickly through the thousands of arcade titles, their screenshots and cabinet art appearing and disappearing in a cascade of gaming history, "this is some old ass software. Back when my man here was younger, all of these games would actually be separate machines, but then someone had the idea of emulating all of this stuff on the PC. Completely awesome, and soooo fucking illegal these days. Randy is probably like the last guy around here to have a working MAME cab like this."

"Cool," said Blake.

"Randy, man, come on, find a game for us!" said Jay with excitement and an obvious buzz.

"How about *The Simpsons Arcade Game*?"

"Done," said Jay, scrolling to the S section and loading the game.

Whereas Jay was a novice when it came to vintage gaming, it was clear that Blake was so unfamiliar with the concept of arcade controls that she did not know which hand to use for the buttons

36

and which for the joystick. Eventually, she made a few pensive pushes of the stick with her left hand and began to methodically press the buttons with her right and observe what effect they had on the game.

"Like this?" she asked.

"Yeah, girl, that's how you work that stick!" said Jay, with a laugh and a poke.

The two made their way through the game's first level, with Jay playing as Homer and Blake as Marge. They giggled as they became familiar with each character's attacks and began to dispatch Smither's goons with speed and skill.

"So, like, this is what you did when you were a kid?" asked Blake.

"Well, arcades were kind of dying by the time I was old enough to go out on my own," said Randy, "but yeah, kids would hang out in these halls and play games like this. Pretty fun, actually."

"What's the history of this one?" asked Jay, as he pounded on the Attack button to win the balloon inflation mini-game.

"This one was a typical side-scroller for the time," said Randy, surprised that his guests were still asking for history lessons. "It was a pretty simple concept. Just a button-masher, really, but it was the artwork that drew kids in. This totally looked like *The Simpsons* cartoon back then. It was part of a long line of Konami beat'em ups. They had an X-men one and a Ninja Turtles game. All four or six player games. You'd just go to the arcade with friends and pump quarters into them and see how far you'd get before you were broke."

"Oh, Konami," said Blake, "they make those fantasy football gambling terminals in our student center!"

"Probably," replied Randy, not knowing exactly to what she was referring, as he had not been on a college campus in many years. "They were actually a pretty prominent company back in the day. They had a lot of great franchises for a number of home consoles, but they ultimately…"

Randy noticed that, as he was going on about Konami, Jay had slipped his hand into the back of Blake's jogging pants and began caressing her in fine strokes underneath the fabric. He figured that this was his cue to grab the last of the beers and give them some space.

He walked over to the Super Nintendo section of his bookshelf, pulled out a copy of *Super Mario All-Stars*, and went over to his console collection. He flicked on the power switch to his massive entertainment center and placed the cartridge into his faded gray and purple SNES. With a pull on the handle of his rotating shelf, he positioned his old Zenith perfectly in front of his couch, and the cheerful intro theme to the famous 1993 remake of the NES Mario games began to play. Finishing the last drops of his beer, he dug through a bin of controllers, plugged one in, and selected the original Super Mario game.

This whole process of spinning the wheel to select the right display and powering on his console collection always made him giddy, especially on nights when the beer was flowing. There was something about the act that seemed powerfully retro, like a combination of spinning the prize wheel on an 80s edition of *The Price is Right* while living within the store shelves of an Electronic Boutique. It was the kind of experience that people did not actually have in the 80s and 90s and was, in fact, only achievable through the zeal, resources, and free time that obsessive collectors had years after the fact, but it felt incredible nonetheless. He reclined back in his tattered couch, rested one foot on the coffee table in front of him, and began making his way through the iconic platformer.

Super Mario All-Stars was, in fact, a rather uninspired choice of a game to play, especially when showing off the game room to people he was trying to initiate into the remnants of retro culture, but it was a game that evoked such strong feelings of contentment and nostalgia that he could not resists it when caught in the midst of a five beer buzz. It was a game released one year after he was born, and he had played it religiously while sitting on the floor in his pajamas and staring up in wonderment at the TV in his parents' living room, once he was old enough to handle a controller. He played it at a time before he could have ever imagined the aneurysm in his mother's head that ended her life or the bullet in his father's head that ended his—a time when the crispness of the buttons and the faint smell of warm electronics promised a future of progress and discovery within the secure and predictable confines of small town American life. He could almost hear the sizzle of the tater-tots and steak sandwiches his mother would make for him on Friday nights as he tried to survive the *Lost Levels*. He could remember the youthful haste to complete his homework so he could return to the Mushroom Kingdom and spend an hour or two lost in these early virtual worlds—worlds which functioned as positive examples of human-machine interaction and represented optimism about the trajectory of technological development. This was not a time when gaming required a persistent Internet connection or the player needed a credit card at the ready to overcome numerous in-game paywalls. Games were pleasurable digital diversions that sought only to offer a fun and brief escape from reality each time the power button was pressed. It was this combination of hope, escapism, and an attachment to his own past that had anchored Randy in the world of retro gaming.

There was, however, another dimension to this nostalgia that made its allure irresistible. People have always been nostalgic in some form or another, yearning for a return to an idyllic past that was forever lost to time, but the nostalgia of retro gaming culture was qualitatively different, in that technology allowed the experience of playing video games to persist through time and remain alive in the present. The devices which facilitated youthful escape in the 90s could, in very many cases, function in exactly the same ways forty years later. Randy could go back to the SNES, pick up the same game, and play the same save file that he created in 1996. He could experience the same games, in the same ways, that he did when he was ten years old, only with greater maturity and discernment. Nostalgia was no longer an impulse to return to an earlier, blissful stage of life that was irrevocably lost, but an actual, lived experience—a continued exploration of a medium that had not been exhausted in its own time. There were thousands of games released between 1985 and 2000, more than any one person could play and, for people like Randy, the constant thrill of discovering something new was a steady invitation to return to the past and continue a journey that was incapable of ever being completed. In the game room, the longevity of technology became a technology of memory, a portal for accessing the experiences of one's virtual past in an attempt to cope with, escape from, or forget the present.

Randy had lost himself in the bright contrast of the azure sky and deep green trees of the remastered levels of *Super Mario Bros.* when Jay plopped down on the couch beside him and threw a small plastic bag onto the coffee table, which contained three syringe-shaped objects.

"Fuck is that?" asked Randy

"Lollipops, bro. Fuckin fun as shit," said Jay, draping his arm over Randy's shoulder. "I never come to a party empty-handed."

"OMG, these are so much fun," said Blake, leaning over the back of the couch, close enough so that Randy could smell her watermelon body splash.

"I've never heard of lollipops. Looks like crack or something," said Randy.

"Better," said Jay, opening the bag and taking out the suspicious objects.

"I don't inject stuff."

"Dude, it really is a fucking lollipop. You aren't injecting anything."

"What is it then?"

"It is basically heroin on a stick," said Jay, popping off the small, curved end of the stick to reveal a red candy that he stuck between his cheek and his gums.

Blake unwrapped her lollipop and took a lick.

"It is actually a lot smoother than heroin. No rush and no crash. It just helps you relax," she said.

Randy reluctantly took the last of the lollipops and unwrapped it. He had never taken any kind of hard drug, as alcohol was usually sufficient for relaxing him. He had smoked some weed in college and tried some THC extract at a bar after cannabis was deregulated, but it didn't appeal to him at all. As he got older, his goal was only to relax and not to chase a physical high, which had become a small pastime for many in the region. In the game room, he wanted only to play games and that required a moderate degree of alertness and precision, which alcohol preserved in the right quantities.

"Come on," whispered Blake into Randy's ear, her face so close to his that he could feel the warmth of her breath with each syllable. "I promise you'll like it."

Randy gave in and stuck the candy into his mouth. His tasted like orange.

"Come on babe, back to gaming!" said Jay, grabbing Blake by the arm and pulling her back to the arcade cabinet. "We gotta beat this fucking game."

"Babe?" said Blake with a laugh. "Are you like a fuckin' old man? Who says that!"

Randy picked up his SNES controller and continued with *Super Mario Bros.*, nervously waiting for whatever drug was in the lollipop to kick in. He had an innate fear of giving up control of his body, and with each passing moment he visualized generic-looking chemical bonds for this unknown substance coursing through his blood and invading his brain. To his surprise, however, he did not lose control of his faculties and could continue playing for quite some time. The effect was not immediate, but rather a delayed, muted euphoria and a growing sense of relaxation that traveled across his body like a ripple of warm water. After about 30 minutes of blissful gameplay, he put the controller down and just enjoyed the iconic underwater music of Level 7-2 of *Super Mario* as it mixed with the faint sounds of oral sex behind him.

4

The morning began with the hum of a vibrating smartphone and a dull pain in Randy's chest. Blake and Jay were long gone and he found himself reclined on the couch in his game room, with *Super Mario All-Stars* on a pause screen. He shifted his weight and got down on one knee, which he used for support as he rose to his feet. He stretched to loosen his muscles a bit and alleviate the pressure pulsating in his core which, while not as sharp as it had been a minute ago, was still uncomfortable.

Randy locked up the game room and headed into his house. Either the lollipops did indeed have a terrible crash or, in combination with the five beers he had consumed, they were contributing to a wretched hangover. He grabbed a glass from the cupboard and walked into the bathroom in an adjacent hallway to get some water, as the sink in the kitchen was filled with old, unwashed dishes that had been collecting there for the past four weeks. As he drank from his old Mega Man coffee mug, he stared at himself in the mirror and confronted the cruel reality that he was aging more than he had realized. When he was in the solitude of the game room, reliving his youth, it was easy to forget his actual age and ignore the gradual signs of unavoidable entropy that were now plainly evident on his face. His eyes were bloodshot and the skin around them was wrinkled. His glasses were old and scratched. A thin white crust had collected in the corners of his mouth, and his hairline had begun to recede since the last time he encountered his reflection.

He filled his mug and took another drink of water—a larger, more forceful gulp, hoping that the face he saw was the temporary result of alcoholic dehydration. As he leaned down to wash up, he felt a painful fullness from the water in his stomach, which gurgled in his chest and pushed back into his mouth, creating a stale and sour taste he had never experienced before. He again tried to stretch his arms high into the air to stop this unpleasant sensation, but the gurgling continued and more water spurted back into his throat and mouth, this time burning his nostrils and causing him to spit the noxious liquid into the sink. He rubbed his chest vigorously, which seemed to help a bit, brushed his teeth, and combed his hair. He was too nauseous to eat.

He prepared a pot of coffee and checked his notifications as he waited for it to brew. $400 had been deposited into his account for the hazardous waste haul, which meant $800 had been subtracted for his lateness and the accident. He was unconcerned, however, as his annuity and his profit sharing deposits would happen soon, and he had two hauls lined up for next week. The next notification was from the city environmental authority, informing him that he would have to be home at 7:30am next Tuesday to have his tap water checked for contamination. This was an inconvenience, because he would have to get up early just to have some city official tell him his drinking water was within contamination tolerance limits, which was the same result he had received for the past 8 years. The last notification was a text from Jay asking him to meet up at the Wyoming Valley Mall at 6:00 pm.

"Dude, MALL! Meet at the food court. Big plans," it read.

As he got up to check the coffee pot, which had an annoyingly slow brewing cycle, it occurred to him, perhaps for the first time, that he was uncomfortable allowing his relationship with Jay to grow any deeper. When he first met him, he saw Jay as a resource because of his technical knowledge and his ability to get his hands on hardware that was not readily available to the average person–a skill that was undoubtedly useful in a time of heavily regulated technology. The fact that he was genuinely interested in retro gaming culture was a plus and, because he lived three streets away, he was always available and just needed an excuse to leave the house. The game room had, in fact, become Jay's hang out of choice– perhaps because Wilkes-Barre offered young people very few meaningful activities or hangouts outside of work, and any stimulus was worth exploring. Or perhaps it was because he wanted to escape sharing a house with his alcoholic mother, who had the reputation of being a kind of on again, off again prostitute who would post to Craigslist looking for casual encounters in exchange for money, liquor or both. In fact, Randy was pretty sure he had used her services several years ago when he met a woman in downtown Wilkes-Barre for a blowjob, which cost him $40 plus a bottle of whiskey. He wasn't fully sure, but there was not a huge pool of people who posted to message boards looking for casual encounters on the edges of the shale fields, so it was a strong probability, and one that, out of guilt, led him to socialize with Jay on a more frequent basis than he would have liked.

There was, however, something about the request to meet up at the mall that bothered him. What big plans could Jay possibly have? Were truly big plans even possible anymore? It felt like he was being pulled into a childish pursuit and he felt very distant from the unrealizable dreams of youth. He wasn't sure what he could offer to a 21-year-old and his girlfriend, outside of a place to drink and fuck, so it therefore didn't make sense that they would want to do something with him in public, and the older he became, the more he tried to actively avoid public spaces. He texted back.

"Big plans? Just email me. Not in the mood."

"Dude, come on," responded Jay.

For a guy who was supposedly very busy with his many gigs, he always had the time to text.

"What're you after?

"Nothin, dude. Me and Blake have this awesome idea. We NEED to see you."

"Fine. What time?"

Randy was feeling too queasy to argue.

"Six."

He filled up a Styrofoam cup with black coffee and added a prodigious amount of milk and sugar. The pain in his chest had subsided a bit and the coffee invigorated him, quelled the unease in his stomach, and chased away the fog from his mind. He looked down at his phone and fired up an Internet browser, at which point he received an error indicating that his monthly Internet quota was about to expire. He didn't want to spend the $100 to boost his limit and just clicked through several pages of warnings to google the Wyoming Valley Mall. He had not been to the mall in years and was surprised to see that it was still open and, thankfully, didn't even have a security check at its entrance. If you wanted to shop in the modern, downtown stretch of stores in Wilkes-Barre, you had to pre-register online for entry, or buy a monthly pass, and then wait in line for a security scan. It was one of the main reasons that he avoided what little night life there was in the city. Had the mall required such a procedure, he would have probably backed out, but it was good to know there were still a few places that allowed you to just show up and shop, like in the old days.

As much as he lacked enthusiasm for learning about Jay's "big plans," he could not suppress a playful wave of nostalgia at the idea of going to the mall, as malls were one of the main avenues for exploring video games in his youth. They were one of the few places where almost every game available could be purchased and where you could catch a glimpse of the latest technology and dream about what the then nascent industry was going to bring to market. He remembered being 7 years old and waiting in the mall for the release of the Sega Dreamcast, which was one of the last nice things his father ever bought for him. He remembered playing *Luigi's Mansion* at a kiosk in a GameStop in 2001 and buying an Xbox 360 at the Software Etc. with money from his first part-time job.

By 2018, most malls in the Corridor region had completely died out, and Randy hadn't even heard the word "mall" mentioned since about this time. Here in the Valley, they had seemed especially obsolete, as the mass exodus of people in the late 2010s and early 2020s left very few residents with the time and resources to shop in physical stores. The longer Randy considered it, it seemed unfathomable that this one mall somehow managed to survive the social upheaval of the past 15 years and exist in a community that had little use for it.

The drive there was familiar, in that it was located not all that far from the depot to which he delivered the drill rods yesterday, albeit on the other side of a massive security perimeter that separated the city's specialized industrial infrastructure from its residential areas. The parking lot seemed to have been used as a staging area for one or more of the construction projects that were always happening on the outskirts of the city, as it was littered with forklifts, steel beams, trailers, and all manner of debris. A network of makeshift signs guided visitors through the construction site and to a small parking lot on the opposite side of the facility, which was similar to the mall parking lots he remembered as a kid. An illuminated white sign flickered the word "Entrance" in red letters above an atrium, which appeared to be the only way into the building.

The mall had a surreal, almost timeless quality to it when he walked through the atrium doors. What stood before him was a silent, spotless monument to the past—an edifice of shiny corridors that was largely unchanged from his childhood memories. There was still an old directory in the foyer, which had severely faded over time but seemed to be from the late-2000s. The east wing of the mall was pitch black and cordoned off with traffic cones and a thin plywood barrier, but the west wing was instantly recognizable. The floors were made of a highly polished faux marble and the railings were of a generic, light colored wood, worn smooth from years of use. Rows of old, but still functioning spherical light bulbs lined the columns that stretched across the hall on both the top and bottom levels, their light mixing with that from the white, opaque skylights above to give the structure a neutral, relaxing glow. The air had a clean, cool, pleasantly antiseptic quality to it that was perfectly suited to any season. Outside of the faint footsteps audible in the distance and the soft, mechanical squealing of escalators rolling up and down in obvious futility, the place was bathed in an ethereal stillness. Most stores were closed, and a few had been converted into office space. The only ones that remained open were two drug stores, a liquor store, and a discount women's clothing store. The mall no longer served a purpose, but here it stood, boldly resisting the realities of the era.

The food court was a little livelier, as it seemed to be functioning as a truck stop for local haulers to grab a quick bite to eat after ending long hauls from deep in the western shale fields. Randy even recognized some of their faces from other rest stops in the Corridor and the long traffic lines that formed around the main security checkpoints during the busiest times of year. Like the mall, the food court had remained unchanged in its appearance, with large, illuminated purple triangles adorning the tops of each stand–likely a late 80s attempt at making this corner of the mall seem futuristic. While the design elements remained stuck in the past, the food offerings had changed significantly. A bibimbap stand had replaced what Randy remembered to be the Orange Julius, and there were multiple Thai food options and a "Panini Center" taking the place of staples like Sbarro's Pizza and Nathan's Hot Dogs. There was one hamburger place left and, for the sake of tradition, Randy decided to order his favorite mall fare: a bacon cheeseburger and chili fries.

Jay and Blake were sitting off in a corner, shoulder to shoulder, watching YouTube videos on Jay's phone. He must have gotten paid, Randy thought, as YouTube subscriptions weren't cheap these days. He guessed that this might have been what passed as a splurge night for younger people–binging on cellular data and eating bad food in public.

"Evening, guys," said Randy, sliding into their booth.

"Hey," said Blake, looking up from the phone with a smile, "It's so awesome that you decided to come. Isn't this place cool?"

"It's kind of dead, actually," said Randy, "I can't believe this place still exists."

Jay looked up from his phone. "Nah, it's still going. Rumor has it they use the mall as a secret interrogation center."

"Come on," said Blake, punching Jay in the shoulder and then leaning in for a cuddle. "You're, like, so into these conspiracy theories."

"No, seriously dude, there's like this whole other abandoned wing. I know this guy who said the cops brought him here for a while. Freaked him the fuck out."

"So, basically, your dealer," replied Blake with a sardonic grin. "*He's* your source."

"I don't name sources."

"What are these big plans?" asked Randy, interrupting what he thought could be one of many flirty exchanges for which he did not have the patience.

"Oh yeah, so Blake and I were thinking. Your fucking game room is awesome. I mean, there's nothing like it within 50 miles of this shithole. Why not show it to the world?"

"What do you mean?" asked Randy.

"Well, you've got like every system, right? Why not do something totally old school and do a stream of the fuckin' history of video games. Play everything you have, give a tour of the room, invite some people over. You know, like a party and shit and people can watch it online," said Jay.

"Yeah," added Blake, "no one does anything cool like that around here. You know so much about this stuff and you basically just lock yourself up in your room. Let's show it to the world! You could be online famous for this!"

Randy gave his companions a puzzled glance. They probably didn't realize that thousands of people had recorded videos about retro gaming and did streams of their collections for the better part of a decade. This form of media had, of course, long since faded into obscurity, so rather than point out their ignorance of the culture, he decided to throw out some other valid reasons to decline.

"Nah, that sort of thing is not for me. First off, I can't afford enough Internet to stream anything and plus, there are gaps in my collection. It really isn't complete."

"Dude, you know I can take care of the Internet stuff and set up the stream. What systems are you missing?"

"Turbo Duo and Virtual Boy," said Randy, "and they are literally fucking impossible to get."

"So let's get'em!" said Blake, with surprising enthusiasm.

"It isn't that simple. You can't just *get* a working Turbo Duo and Virtual Boy these days. They're the rarest of the rare and I'm almost certain they don't exist anywhere around here."

"First off, that isn't true," said Jay. "I know a guy who lives in the fuckin' boon docks and he's got the biggest hardware inventory of anyone in this area—even you."

"You mean that Dave the Collector guy?" Randy said. "He's a nut job who rants and raves on the Internet all day. I bet he doesn't have half the stuff he says he does."

"He does," Jay assured him. "I use him as a supplier for some stuff. He lives on this farm or some shit way down south, outside of Intercourse. He's got this massive shed filled with gear you won't find anywhere else. I'm not sayin' he's got these two things you're looking for, but he'll know where to find them."

"Even so," said Randy with hesitation, "why would people care about this? Who's going to watch us? I'm not losing money on a stream."

"I told you," said Jay, "I have a way to stream this shit for free. I've got contacts. Seriously, no one even remembers this stuff and you've got this museum full of it. Let's get famous off of that shit."

Randy again felt an uncomfortable gurgling in his chest and leaned back to help alleviate it. "And why is this so important to you guys?"

"I guess," said Jay, "I don't know. I guess maybe 'cause we'll never meet another guy like you. With all the knowledge and the history and stuff. And this could be really big. It's like..."

"Because you can share your passion with the world," said Blake. "Doesn't that mean anything to you? These days no one does anything just for the sake of it. No one really celebrates anything. And we can do it right here. We can do something meaningful right here in the middle of this disgusting city."

"Well," said Randy, certain that they would not let him say no and surprised at their sustained enthusiasm, "I guess I can think about it. I don't know if I like the idea of a party but we can definitely think about a stream...IF it's not going to cost me."

"Sweet. You won't regret this, bro" said Jay offering up a fist bump.

"I promise this'll be fun and plus, you'll finally land these two systems you need to complete your collection," said Blake. She said this looking down and toward Jay's phone, but Randy felt her foot caress the inside of his thigh and punctuate the sentence with an assuring scrunch of her toes. It was the first time a woman had touched him in months.

After dinner, the group decided to walk the empty halls of the mall. In the past, such a pursuit could occupy hours of pleasant idleness but, as there was nothing open except the mall itself, they became bored.

"Alright, I'm taking off," said Randy after they looped back around to the food court.

"Come on, man, the night is young," replied Jay.

"There's fuckin' nothing to do. I'm out," said Randy.

"It is kind of pathetic after a while," said Blake, grabbing Jay's hand.

"I've got an idea. Let's go to the abandon section. Let's see what shit really goes on there!" suggested Jay.

"Uh, maybe they didn't teach you this in your tech training for the city," said Randy, "but they give you like a ten grand fine for trespassing and if you can't pay it, you're gonna wind up in one of those correction centers."

"It's not trespassing. We're in the fucking mall, so what if we wander around?" said Jay.

With that, he darted off toward the east wing of the mall. Randy and Blake shouted after him, but he refused to stop and disappeared into the darkness. They didn't immediately follow him, as they were nervous that their shouting would attract security personnel, but as the echoes of their words faded and the stillness of the mall returned, they decided to pursue him.

They reached the traffic cones and the plywood barrier, which Randy stopped to survey. He saw that the bottom right corner of the plywood could be pulled back and it seemed that this is where Jay had entered the abandoned wing, so he yanked it back as much as he could and motioned to Blake to crawl through it. He followed, snaking his body around the narrow opening and groaning in pain as the barrier snapped back into place and hit him in the chest.

"Are you ok?" asked Blake, rushing over to him.

"Fine," replied Randy in a half-grunt, pulling himself through to the other side.

They found themselves in a pitch black corridor, which they could only navigate by the light of their smartphones. Randy went first, shining his screen in front of him and Blake followed, holding on to the bottom of his leather coat and shining her phone at the ground and to the sides, which revealed shuttered storefronts with rusting security grates. Thirty yards ahead, they came upon a chain link fence, attached to a second sheet of plywood, through which a door had been cut. Randy pushed it open and they entered another atrium, which was half-illuminated by flickering, spherical lightbulbs. Jay sat laughing on the remnants of a children's carousel.

"Isn't this cool?" he asked.

"Yeah, what is this place?" asked Blake.

"This is the mall, dude!" said Jay.

Although Randy found it odd that this abandoned section of the mall would still have its lights turned on, it was far from a secret police interrogation center. If the wing of the mall in which they had eaten was a monument to a past era, this section was a time capsule—completely neglected for an untold number of years. Grass had begun to push up through the tiles. There was a thick layer of dust on every surface, and a tree, which had been planted in the center of the atrium, had grown so uncontrollably over the years that its roots had smashed up through the floor and its branches had extended to obscure the second-level hallways. The glass on many of the storefronts was shattered and some of the security grates on the stores had been lifted up or removed, revealing mounds of sleeping bags and other used camping equipment, as if the stores had, at one point, been occupied by squatters.

"I got a challenge," said Jay. "We're goin' on a scavenger hunt. 30 minutes. We go into these stores and search for shit. Whoever finds the coolest thing is the winner."

"Are you sure about this?" asked Blake with a hint of worry.

"I'm tellin' you," said Jay, "There's no one here. Let's have fun!"

Jay ran off and ascended a broken escalator to the second level. Blake remained and looked at Randy, certain that she did not want to play the game on her own but unsure of whom she should follow. Her large, soulful green eyes again revealed signs of a deep sadness that seemed to be always pulsating under the surface of her delightful ease of being. She began to walk backwards with ever increasing pace, then turned and ran up the escalator, imploring Jay to wait for her.

Randy stood in the atrium for a minute and stared at his phone. 9:30pm. This was not good. What they were doing was very much illegal and could have dire consequences for all of them, but there was something about the mall that allayed his typical paranoia. For the entire time they had been there, they had not seen one cop or private security officer. There were no signs of security cameras and no patrol drones, which Jay, in his obsessive scanning, would have pointed out. In a city that had no invisible spaces outside of the precarious privacy of one's own home, this mall seemed, by some inexplicable coincidence, to fall outside of society's gaze.

Randy nonetheless decided to stay on the first floor of the atrium, close to the door through which they had entered, and walked into the most accessible store front, which was empty, save for a few pieces of shelving that were piled up near the entrance. In the back of the store, he noticed a rather large hole, as if someone had smashed through the wall with a sledgehammer to access the adjacent space. He walked through it and found a slightly larger shop, with 5 rows of shelves and a display case and cash register to the right of the opening. He bent down to inspect the carpeting, which required brushing away years of caked-on dust, and noticed that it was blue with specks of neon colors arranged in a haphazard pattern. In the center of the store was a group of white wireframe bins of the kind used to house old bulk or discount items. Randy looked inside to find that they were almost empty, save for a large, crinkled piece of paper on the bottom of one of them. He took it over to the display case and tried to flatten it out. With the help of his phone, he made out the faded image of Bill Goldberg, an old pro wrestler he remembered from his very earliest days of watching TV. The man was screaming and the word "Mayhem" was written below his chin.

Randy then proceeded to inspect the aisles of shelving, most of which were empty, with the exception of a few screw drivers and broken item hooks that had been left behind. The front of each shelf and the running boards near the ceiling of the room were, like the carpet, a faded shade of blue, and he shined his phone toward them, hoping to find inscriptions that might give him a clue as to what the store used to be. After searching for a bit, he heard an eerie crunch of plastic beneath his left shoe and jumped back. He pointed his phone light downward to discover that he had stepped on what looked to be a plastic toy, still in its box. He dusted off the packaging, revealing it to be a Superman action figure. On the top right-hand corner of the box he saw a faded sticker, which read "KayBee Clearance: $7.95."

He ran again to the counter with a childlike glee, realizing that he was walking through the remains of one of the stores that had defined his youth. The counter upon which he was inspecting his find was the same counter from which, decades earlier, he stared up in amazement at a Playstation 2 that was locked away in a display case with a multi-colored PS logo that, from a child's perspective, seemed impossibly distant. For a child under ten, one of the monumental abilities that adults possessed was the power to make those games and systems escape from their glass security cases and descend into the hands of expectant children. KayBee Toys seemed to have existed for this specific purpose, so that kids, after having spent a day trying on school clothes or watching their parents shop for curtains, could beg their moms and dads to enact that magic, to disappear with them into the colorful aisles of densely packed toys and video games and emerge with some small pleasure that would produce an intense sensation of early consumer bliss.

Randy wanted to remain in the store and reflect on the many such moments of happiness he had had there, particularly with his mother, who in her attempts to ameliorate the sting of his parents' divorce, would spoil him with small toys and cheap games. That he could have a similar sensation now, 24 years later—judging by the 2006 copyright mark on the Superman box—was remarkable and almost unthinkable. This mall could have been, and probably should have been, demolished years ago, but yet he was able to get one more toy from KayBee, to have one last moment of innocent excitement amidst the pale dust that swirled in the light of his phone.

Randy exited the store to find Jay and Blake waiting by the carousel. They were again immersed in some videos on Jay's smartphone.

"What did you guys find?" asked Randy.

"Hey dude, unbelievable" said Jay, pulling out some industrial cabling from a bag he had found, "old CAT-5s, HDMIs and some old component cables. Pretty sweet. What about you?"

"Just this," said Randy, showing his friends the Superman action figure, "found it in what used to be an old toy store. Can't believe it survived all these years."

"Awesome, man," said Jay, nudging Blake, who pulled out a ream of old, blank movie tickets.

"I guess you guys win," she said with a smile.

The group then proceeded to enter a store on the opposite side of the atrium, behind the carousel, in which Jay had scouted an exit to the mall and, once outside, found themselves at least a mile away from the parking lot, lost in a maze of rusting construction equipment. They were hesitant to activate the GPS function on their phones, for fear of providing evidence that they were trespassing, so they huddled together and crept forward through the icy air of the late autumn evening, eventually scaling a concrete barricade to get back to the main parking lot, which was now empty. Although the grounds were devoid of all signs of human activity, it felt very different from the peculiar stillness of the mall which, while threatening at first, had grown to become a kind of temporary refuge. The silence of the parking lot was firmly rooted in the reality of Wilkes-Barre, which they could see from the mall property as a shadowy mass on the horizon, behind which the constant glow of the shale fields extended into the sky.

5

The Nintendo Virtual Boy was known as Nintendo's only failed console. It was a red visor which rested upon a cheap tripod and promised to immerse players in the first commercially viable, virtual worlds. In reality, it used two cheap, red LED screens to create monochromatic graphics with various layers of parallax scrolling that simulated 3D environments. It was ostensibly portable, but had terrible battery life and required tethering oneself to an outlet to achieve longer play sessions. It only had one controller which, while comfortable, also housed the battery pack or the AC power pack, meaning that weight and wires disrupted its sense of balance. The device also had the reputation of being exceedingly uncomfortable to play, and was reported to have given a large percentage of users neck aches, blurred vision, and nausea.

The system only had fourteen official games released in North America before being discontinued in 1996. In the mid-to-late 2000s, those steeped in retro culture began to remember it fondly as an innovative, if ill-conceived, piece of gaming history. As a result, prices for the system and the games rose on the secondhand market, putting it out of reach for many collectors. Around the same time, its electronics began to fail, creating graphical banding issues that made games unplayable. This led to a so-called perfect storm of rarity for functional units, which continued into 2030, such that locating a working Virtual Boy was an exceedingly rare occurrence and, in the few instances that working units were discovered, they had commanded a price beyond the budgets of most collectors.

It would therefore be a gargantuan task for Randy to acquire a working Virtual Boy and stage Jay and Blake's night of gaming history. He didn't have the money to pay for it outright and didn't have access to credit or any kind of payday advance which he could use to acquire the system, so he bit the bullet and contacted the reclusive hardware enthusiast known as Dave the Collector. Dave had used YouTube and various Internet forums to portray himself as a kind of right-wing mad scientist who was using his tech know-how to plot the overthrow of the government, but seemed to Randy as nothing more than a pitchman for various custom-made computers and other gadgets that he allegedly built at a farm outside of Intercourse, Pennsylvania. It thus seemed quite suspicious when, within 5 minutes of Randy sending him a private message about his desire to acquire a Virtual Boy on a Nintendo Collectors Forum, Dave responded with a trade proposal: One working Virtual Boy for one working LaserDisc player. While LaserDisc players were themselves quite rare in working condition, there was very little demand for them. If you sold a working Virtual Boy, however, you could source and buy a LaserDisc player with just a fraction of the profits. Nonetheless, as Randy did have a working Pioneer CLD-D703 player, he felt compelled to at least meet up with Dave and see if he was for real.

The meeting was to take place at his infamous farm outside of the state's Amish settlements, one of the few places in Pennsylvania that was completely outside the influence of the Energy Corridor and also far enough away from Philadelphia to have retained a modicum of independence. It was located on a road that connected Intercourse, Pennsylvania to the small town of Gap, and driving there was a shocking experience for Randy. Although he was used to traversing vast expanses of Pennsylvania countryside in his work as a hauler, that work always occurred within the Corridor, which had a way of blending nature and heavy machinery such that there was not a stretch of it that could be called rural in the traditional sense. Even in the few areas devoid of workers and drills, there were transport pipes for natural gas and miles of high speed highways branching off in all directions. The road to Gap, on the other hand, was desolate but livable. There were farms every few miles, with people still living and working on them in a bucolic splendor that seemed almost artificial. He even came upon an Amish caravan and saw them in their traditional 18th century attire. It seemed amazing that the Amish managed to resist the inexorable thrust of progress that had transformed the rest of the state, but here they were, traveling their trading routes as they had for hundreds of years.

Dave the Collector's farm was set off from the road by a long dirt driveway littered with tree branches and leaves. When Randy arrived, he was greeted by five aggressive dogs who stood in front of his car and produced a cacophony of violent barking. Their teeth were sharp, their bodies slender, and three had badly scarred faces with missing eyes. Randy reached for his phone to ring Dave, but before he completed the call, a shirtless man, gaunt and sunburned, shewed the dogs to the side and approached the truck.

"You must be Randy!" he said, flashing a toothless, ironic smile through his knotty beard. "Welcome to paradise."

He stretched his arms out and spun in a circle before doubling forward in laughter.

"Are you Dave?" asked Randy in an irrepressibly dyspeptic tone.

"The fuck else would I be, man!"

"I don't know. You look different from your videos," said Randy, grabbing the LaserDisc player from the passenger seat in the hopes of getting the deal done quickly.

"Hahahaha. Those videos. Those videos...Yeah. YEAH. I mean, does anyone still watch those things?"

"Some of us in the community do, I guess," said Randy.

"Well, I hope they're still entertaining. Cause I entertained myself makin' em and I moved a ton of gear with them," said Dave, crossing his arms and staring at the LaserDisc player.

"Yeah, well, I wanna see that Virtual Boy. Where do you keep it?" asked Randy, sickened by the smell of labor, sun, and sweat emanating from Dave's pores—an odor that was surprising given the crisp fall weather.

"You givin' me orders, man? On my fuckin' farm. Come on. You gotta do better than that."

"Do better than what?"

"Than fuckin' treatin' me like some dumb hick" said Dave. "Who the fuck are you, man? I mean, I'm doin' ya a favor here, man. I know how much that Virtual Boy is worth. I could fuckin' sell that thing tomorrow to some rich hedge fund douchebags in London or Vancouver or New York who would pay me a shit-ton for it. But I'm not. I'm tradin' with ya because I hate the types of bastards that could afford it. I'm doin' ya a solid, brother."

"Look, I didn't mean to offend you," said Randy, unsure of how to follow up because he knew Dave was right and that he couldn't base his aversion to the man on anything other than irritation at his shrill voice and penetrating stench.

"Damn straight. I mean, look, you should be grateful. Grateful for everything, man. Just fuckin' grateful."

"Grateful? Look, I appreciate it" said Randy. "It's a great deal. I apologize, what else do you want me to say?"

"See that? Again, that's a fuckin' pissy response."

"Sorry," said Randy, trying to inflect the word with a hint of emotion, as he suspected Dave was trying to find a way to back out of the deal.

"You even know what you should be grateful for?" asked Dave with a grin.

"To you. For hooking me up."

"Man, you fuckin' kids today. Just programmed to be selfish. Lookin' to screw your fellow man. That's how they're educatin' ya in the system. That's part of the plan. They trap you in a mindset of selfishness and watch as you fuckin' destroy society."

"Look, I said I was sorry. I'm not part of some conspiracy theory. I just wanna get this deal done."

"Real funny, kid. Real funny...I ain't no conspiracy theorist. I mean, maybe I was, but it's no fun anymore. It was better back in the days when there was still a difference between a conspiracy theory and a business plan. These days any old asshole with half a brain can come up with some crazy story and, chances are, it's probably true! Now just follow me, brother," said Dave, grabbing Randy by the arm and dragging him towards a dirt path.

Randy felt himself growing ever angrier at Dave's real life personality, which was harder to tolerate than the character he played online. On the Internet, Dave was nothing more than a stereotypical salesman and a right-wing self-promoter, a kind of person who, while irritating, seemed very straight forward to deal with if you had the money. In person, however, he was irascible and subtly condescending in a way that unsettled Randy at a visceral level. He had hoped to be on and off of the farm with his prize in hand, but Dave seemed to be exploiting the fact that the deal was happening on his turf and that there was not another working Virtual Boy within two-hundred miles of his property.

Randy followed Dave for about a quarter mile until they came upon a huge metal storage barn next to a barren field. Dave punched a code into a keypad and pulled open a heavy, metal door to reveal a massive warehouse of machinery and exotic technology. On a table in front of one of the mile-deep rows of electronics sat a Virtual Boy. It had been turned on and the music to *Mario's Tennis* was echoing off of the steal walls.

"This is what you want, right?" said Dave, directing Randy to the table with the exaggerated gesture of a French waiter in a Saturday morning cartoon.

"Holy shit," said Randy, "yeah, this is it."

He walked over to the table, put the Laserdisc player on the floor, sat down, and peered into the system, which was in immaculate condition, to the point that the neoprene face-protector smelled just as he remembered it when he demoed the system at a Blockbuster Video in 1995. The buttons were crisp and the graphics showed no hint of the infamous horizontal distortions that signified its immanent failure.

Playing *Mario's Tennis* was a revelation, as it had an instantly recognizable charm and the tight play mechanics that represented the best of what Nintendo offered to its legions of fans in the late 80s and throughout the 90s. As a kid, Randy had actually found the game to be underwhelming compared to other Nintendo releases of the time, but now the cheerful character sprites and the intricately layered backgrounds of the Mushroom Kingdom produced a familiar, nostalgic urge, which was the fuel for the obsessive collecting that defined the entirety of his adult life. He knew he had to have it, which made him nervous, because he assumed there would be some catch that Dave would introduce into the deal.

"Incredible," said Randy, "This is exactly what I was looking for."

"I may be some toothless old man who rants and raves on the net, but, brother, I deliver when I say I am going to deliver," said Dave, exuding the confidence of someone used to having the upper hand in business transactions.

"So you wanna test out the LD player?" asked Randy, assuming that the catch would come at the conclusion of this question.

"Sure," said Dave, grabbing the player off the ground and plugging it into an old CRT TV that he had set up for the meeting. He inspected the hulking, glossy black box with an intense scrutiny that was almost comical.

"Nice. Pioneer CLD series. Both Sides play. Separate CD tray. Remote included. Very Promising."

He played a *DiscoVision* demo disc that he pulled out from a box underneath the TV, which played with incredible graininess and distorted sound. He then stuck in a copy of *Aliens*, which was of much better quality.

"Well, it passed the test of shit and gold," he said to Randy, who was beginning to pack up the Virtual Boy.

"So we have a deal then?"

"No, we don't have a deal."

Randy cringed as the catch he feared had materialized.

"What's wrong? I thought the deal was the LD player for the Virtual Boy?" asked Randy.

Dave walked over to him, stood about an inch from his face, and stared into his eyes.

"I didn't like your apology," he said.

Randy stared back at him for as long as he could, before averting his eyes to the ground as his discomfort grew. He was unsure about what to say or what Dave really wanted, and in his panic began to stutter something that was barely comprehensible, at which point Dave broke out with squealing laughter.

"I am fuckin' with ya, brother. Come on. You were starin' like I'm some kind of a psychopath."

"I don't know, man, you seemed pretty fucking serious" said Randy with nervous laughter.

"Look, I do have a condition, though. You gotta watch a LaserDisc with me and smoke a joint. That's how you make up for treatin' me like garbage there in the beginning."

Randy hesitated. He didn't want to spend one more moment at the farm than was necessary, but he couldn't turn his back on the deal now.

"Yeah, sure. What've you got to watch?" asked Randy.

"Somethin' real special. Come back to the house with me and you'll see."

They made their way up a second branching dirt path to an old farmhouse that looked as if it had been damaged in a storm and abandoned some time before the 1970s. It had a porch cluttered with old magazines in rotting wooden bookshelves. Several of the windows were broken and had black garbage bags taped over the sections where the panes had shattered. The siding was covered in a thick layer of dirt and was beginning to peel off of the house. The only evidence of the modern era was a small solar field in the front yard that was connected to a grid on the left side of the structure by a few dangling wires.

"Make yourself at home," said Dave, gesturing to two chairs on the porch before disappearing through the front door.

Randy moved a mound of wires and rusted circuit boards from one of the chairs, which had a weathered vinyl cover with dandelions in a grid pattern, reminiscent of something he had seen in his grandmother's apartment as a child. To the right of the chairs was another old CRT TV resting atop a broken refrigerator. As dirty and uncomfortable as the porch was, it offered a view of a broad ploughed field and a thicket of deep evergreen trees in the distance, which gave Randy a moment of repose from his paranoid considerations of why Dave had entered the house and left him out here by himself.

The front door eventually swung open and Dave emerged with two joints in his left hand and the LaserDisc player and a disc clutched under his right arm. He handed the joints to Randy and connected the player to the TV via composite video ports hidden behind a plastic cover on the front of the monitor. He plugged it into a massive extension cord that ran into the house and turned it on, seemingly pleased that it was working in its new location. He then grabbed the LaserDisc, spun around, and pushed it in Randy's face.

"You ever seen this, brother?" asked Dave.

It was volume 1 of an old anime called *Bubblegum Crisis*.

"Not in a long, long time," replied Randy, still expecting his host to pull out a weapon of some sort.

"Fuckin' classic."

He popped in the disc, sat in his chair, and lit up both joints, handing one to Randy with a nod.

"Thanks," said Randy, taking a shallow, exploratory drag.

"That's the best stuff you'll get around here. Totally organic. Non-GMO. I sell the shit to a couple of organic shops in Philly and New York. You'd probably pay fifty bucks for something like this up there."

Dave reclined back on his chair, rested one leg on the porch railing to his side, and took a hit from his joint. Randy observed his sunburned skin stretch over his craggy ribs as he held in the drag and then slowly blew it out in a puff of thick, sweet smoke. His head was nodding with increasing intensity to the synth guitar notes of the show's opening theme song, and he was singing along, alternating between moans and broken Japanese.

"So is this how you fund your collection? Selling weed?" asked Randy in an attempt to force an end to this uncomfortable karaoke.

Dave turned his head and gave him another toothless grin, his eyes now reddened and puffy. "Partly. The way I see it, I'm retired and this is one of my sidelines. A hobby really."

"I mean, that warehouse of yours is amazing" continued Randy. "It doesn't look to me like you're completely retired."

"You tryin' to learn my secrets? Why don't you work on that blunt and I'll tell you more?"

Randy took another drag. He could feel a bit of tension fading from his arms and legs, which was a welcomed sensation that made being in Dave's company somewhat more tolerable.

"Sorry, man. I didn't mean to pry," said Randy.

"Well, I'll tell you what man. I'm getting' out of games. I mean, totally fuckin' done. I used to trade'em till I got something rare and then sell that shit. Same with hardware trades. But there's no fucking point anymore. I'm into weed cause I like to garden. And I tinker with newer shit for clients who are tryin' to go underground. You know, people who want a phone or computer and don't want Uncle Sam's pryin' eye up their asshole."

Randy was tempted to ask if he had other gaming merchandise he wanted to unload, but felt like he shouldn't press his luck. The Virtual Boy would be the score of a lifetime, if and when he could get off the farm.

"Yeah, a buddy of mine has used you for some stuff. A guy named Jay. Also from Wilkes-Barre. Young guy." said Randy.

"Hmmm...I deal with so many young guys lookin' to fuck the system, you know. Lot a you types from around that fucking Corridor, actually."

Dave began to puff on his joint with greater intensity. He reached into the broken refrigerator and pulled out a half-finished bottle of whiskey, took a swig and offered some to Randy, who declined. He then leaned back again and began to stare at the anime with disturbing concentration.

"Which one of these girls would you fuck?" he asked. "And don't say Priss. Everyone says Priss."

"I guess the older one," said Randy, unsure of himself.

"Sylia. Nice choice. Great fuckin' rack."

Randy glanced down at the time counter on the LaserDisc player to see that 15 minutes had passed. The weed, though settling him a bit, did nothing to subdue his desire to leave. The typical anime episode was around a half hour, he remembered, and he began counting down the minutes until he would have his freedom.

"You ever figure out why you should be grateful?" asked Dave, turning to him and giving him another sustained, condescending stare.

"Like I said before, I'm grateful that you're giving me this deal. I really appreciate it."

"Man, you are fuckin' thick, brother. You don't fuckin' get it, man. Here you are, on my fuckin' farm, pickin' up a sweet piece of gear for your collection. On a fuckin' Tuesday! I guess you city folks don't know what it means to be grateful."

"City folks? Who exactly do you think I am?" said Randy, no longer able to contain his irritation. "I live in Wilkes-Barre. I'm a fuckin' hauler!"

"Yeah...And you can still afford to live in a city, and take a day off on a Tuesday, and come to my farm and get fuckin pissed at me cause I'm tryin' to have a nice conversation with ya before you run off with your rare score. I mean, you can still fuckin' game, brother! You're a dyin' breed."

"Have you been to Wilkes-Barre?" asked Randy in protest. "The place is a ghost town! I mean, come on, stop treating me like I'm some sort of elitist."

Dave jumped out of his seat in indignation, wobbling and bracing himself against the refrigerator.

"You *are* a fuckin' elitist, brother! I mean, shit, you know all the people who pass through here? People who're kicked out of Washington, New York, or Philly. People ain't got the skills to do anything meaningful in the 'Creative Progress Centers.' They pass through here in their beat up 2014 Dodge Caravans. Headin' south to avoid the energy settlements in this state, loopin' from the Gulf Coast into Mexico to avoid the energy fields in Texas, where they won't even let you drive through without a hassle. Girls staying south of the border to whore themselves out and earn enough dough to make it to California, where at least you can get a job in a fuckin Starbucks or a call center or some shit."

"Yeah, that all fuckin' sucks," yelled Randy, "but what the fuck does it have to do with me?

"Don't you fuckin' get it?" asked Dave, punching one of the banisters on the porch, causing some wood to splinter off and hit the TV screen. "You're it, brother! You're the fuckin' middle class! Well, you and me. I sell weed to hipsters and off-the-grid smartphones to vagrants. You, well, I don't know what the fuck you do. You haul shit and collect games.

Yeah, you live in a city that's got polluted air and poisoned water. But guess what? You live there. In a house. You got some money in your pocket. You're gonna go home and play Virtual Boy. I'm gonna sit here on this porch and jerk off to a cartoon. Like I said, welcome to paradise, brother!"

At this point, Randy didn't know how to respond to Dave's reproaches, so he stood up and handed him the Virtual Boy.

"Look, if you want to cancel the deal, that's fine, just give me the LD player back and I'm gonna fuckin' take off," said Randy.

Dave laughed, turned around, and stared at the TV screen. It was the climactic battle between humans in mech suits and rogue cyborgs looking to take over Tokyo. He grabbed his bottle of whiskey and finished it with an impossibly long swig, letting the empty bottle linger on his lips as he tongued the plastic dispenser for the last, hidden drops of alcohol. Once satisfied that he had extracted all of the Jack Daniels he could, he tossed the empty bottle into the yard, turned to Randy, and hugged him.

"I'm fifty-six years old, man" he said, eventually releasing his grip and stepping back, his arms extended and his hands resting on Randy's shoulders. "I saw this show when I was fifteen. I guess I'm pissed that the world ain't as simple as tits and robots anymore. I'm not backin' out, brother. Take that Virtual Boy and enjoy it. Love it. It's the last of its kind."

Randy walked back to his truck with the Virtual Boy in hand. Each step he took towards the Tundra seemed like an eternity, as he could hear Dave's uncoordinated footsteps following behind him, and couldn't shake the feeling that something bad could still happen. Randy put his prized system in the car and turned around once again to face his host, who threw a small Ziploc bag into his hands.

"Let me know if you need anything else, brother," said Dave, doing a mocking military salute before making his way back up the driveway.

Randy got into his truck and inspected the package, which contained all fourteen North American Virtual Boy games. Shocked by this act of generosity, he watched Dave saunter back onto the porch, light another joint, and recline in front of the TV, the light of which bounced off of his face as he sat there, transfixed in a state of childlike amusement that, at his age, was unintentionally tinged with a soft, hopeless melancholy.

Randy woke up from a night of restless sleep with an uncontrollable cough. He sat up, hung his legs over the edge of the bed, and began gasping for air. His chin was quivering, his cheeks felt numb, and there was a tight knot of pain in his chest. He tried inhaling deeply and regularly to calm himself, but a wave of nausea overcame him and he began heaving into his pillow, eventually producing a thick, pink pus that was absorbed by the fabric of his pillowcase. He scrambled to the bathroom and gulped a glass of water from the faucet, but he again felt the now all too common sensation of gurgling in his chest, which forced him to vomit once again. The result was now a thinner mixture of pink pus and water that spun away in thin, ropey strands into the drain. He opened the bathroom window and collapsed on the floor, drawing in the cold morning air in an attempt to quell the pain and subdue the urge to cough.

He was able to sleep a bit in the bathroom and woke up an hour later with his body under control, though his mind felt fogged and he was unsteady on his feet. Sickness, particularly of an unexplained nature, was a foreign experience in his life. Aside from the common ailments of childhood, he had avoided major illnesses and, despite a lifestyle wanting in nutritious food, he got enough regular exercise at his job to preserve a modicum of physical fitness. It was for this reason that he was never concerned about his health. He assumed hauling would keep him fit into old age and that his genetic constitution was such that he didn't need to go for regular check-ups or simple medical interventions when he was afflicted with the occasional sinus infection or cold. It was, therefore, concerning to him that this chest pain and the gurgling deep within his body seemed to be worsening. He considered researching his symptoms on the Internet, but didn't want to spend the money to access the medical assistance websites, which sat behind expensive paywalls and charged by the minute. If he was going to spend money, he thought that he should seek out a real doctor.

Finding a doctor, however, had become increasingly difficult over the past few years. There were very few private medical practices left in the city, as health care professionals were one of the first groups to leave the region during the first major exodus from Wilkes-Barre a decade ago. The independent practices that did remain were very expensive and were usually contracted to treat employees of the various companies who were housed in the nearby settlements within the Corridor. If you could afford an appointment with them, you would have to wait a month or more to be seen. Most residents had the choice of going to the local hospital or the rehabilitation centers, both of which were free or cheap, thanks to government subsidies, but had the reputation of being very slow to diagnose and treat patients. Once you were in their system, both in the physical and digital sense, you could not leave until you were "stabilized" or "rehabilitated," which in some cases could take weeks or months.

The other option was to make an appointment with the local Wal-Mart Health Center, which was one of many small, acute care practices that began to spring up inside of Wal-Mart stores over the past five years. They claimed to have doctors on call for eighteen hours a day and could supposedly treat a variety of conditions at very reasonable prices. Randy chose this option, as it was quick and he could pick up whatever medications were necessary right at the pharmacy.

He checked-in online and arrived at Wal-Mart shortly after 10:00am. There was a placard at the entrance directing people to the health center, which was located between the bakery and the pharmacy at the far end of the store. He punched his check-in number into a tablet at an informational kiosk, which opened a security door that led to the waiting room.

The room was small, half-full and—though it had a depressing, institutional aura—was clean and bright in a way that few buildings in Wilkes-Barre were. There was no receptionist, but several signs informing patients to have their online check-in info visible on their smartphone screens. He shared the room with an obese man whose hand was wrapped in a bath towel and who seemed to be applying inconsistent pressure to a large wound. There were two elderly couples who sat in a dazed, weary silence, and a Hispanic mother and her two children. Her son was older and sat on the floor with a children's book, thumbing through its colorful pages in mild amusement and stopping at times to describe certain pictures to his sister, who sat on his mother's thigh and seemed to be in a state of pain and fatigue. The little girl's feet were covered in a bright red rash that extended to her ankles and stood in disturbing contrast to her otherwise soft, olive skin. She sat rubbing her pointer and index fingers against her gums and burying her head in the crease between her mother's fleshy shoulder and breast.

One by one, the waiting room began to clear out, and eventually it was Randy's turn. He was called into the office by a young Asian doctor named Xie, who led him down a small hallway to an examination room which, like the waiting area, was bright, modern, and clean. She instructed him in very tentative and imprecise English to sit down at an old Dell desktop computer and complete a "Treatment Form," which asked for his insurance information and then offered him three treatment options priced, presumably, based on what his insurance would cover.

The first option, which cost $79.99 and was called "Healthy Choice," offered Randy a consultation with the doctor and a provisional diagnosis, along with any prescription medications that might be necessary. For $469.99, he could add an onsite diagnostic study (an X-Ray, Ultrasound, or CT scan, as needed) which would be read within three hours and, if warranted, he would receive free transportation to a medical center. The premium option, called "Healthy Choice Premiere," cost $765.99 and included all of the services in the two cheaper plans, plus a one-hour turnaround time on diagnostic studies and a video conference call with a specialist who would offer a guaranteed diagnosis.

Randy chose the cheapest option, as he didn't want to waste his money and felt a desire to evade the subtle paranoia that crept into his mind when he visualized what the diagnostic tests might entail. He entered his bank account info and was forced to click through several pages of warnings and terms and conditions. When he finally submitted all of his info, the interface faded to a white background with an estimated wait time of twenty minutes, which ticked down in the center of the screen.

To break up the monotony of the wait, he took out his smartphone and paid for ten minutes of in-store WiFi, which he used to research prices for the TurboDuo, the last system he needed to complete his collection and move forward with the gaming history livestream. Sadly, Dave did not have one in his collection and claimed not to know of anyone within 50 miles who owned the hardware. There were some niche auction sites that claimed to have working examples, but the prices started at $7,000 and topped off at $20,000 for a unit that came in its original box. Getting his hands on this system would likely be beyond what luck or circumstance could offer him and, to buy it outright, he would need an amount of money that he didn't have and to which he would never have access. As the time ticked away on his WiFi session, he got a text from Blake. It read:

"Meet me! 6:00pm. Monroe and Linden Str. Jesus Statue. Uni Scranton."

The sense of confusion and anticipation that this text produced distracted Randy so much that he did not notice Dr. Xie's modesty knock and was surprised to see her enter the room. She sat down, pulled out a tablet, and began to read off the information that Randy entered in the online appointment form. She was moderately attractive and younger than Randy had anticipated, perhaps no older than 30. Her fit appearance and the barely visible curvature of her body beneath her bright, white coat were enough to make Randy feel self-conscious for sitting there in tattered jeans and a sweater with an abstract sketch of the tri-force from the *Legend of Zelda* series.

There was, however, a subtle nervousness to her demeanor. She operated her tablet with hard taps and an incredulous stare, as if she was unsure if the device would function properly without her firm, authoritative inputs. Her hands shook as she took a tongue depressor and scope cover down from the top shelf of a cabinet. Randy wondered whether this nervousness was linguistic in nature, or if it had its origins in some gap in her professional qualifications— an anxious thought which quickened his pulse and caused a knot to form in his throat.

He tried to break the ice a bit.

"Looked pretty busy in there," he said, with the faintest hint of a smile.

She did not respond.

He cleared his throat and was stung by this small reminder of the social awkwardness of which he was capable, and how this was a potentially damning omen for the invitation he had just received.

"So, you seem to have pains in the chest," Dr. Xie eventually said, nodding as she spoke in a way that hinted at a difficulty both in pronouncing and understanding the words she was saying.

"Yes," said Randy, relieved that he did not need to attempt any more small-talk.

He went on to describe the nature of his pain, when it began, how long the episodes lasted, their varying intensity, their connection to food, and the coughing episode from this morning. There was a certain pleasure in communicating all of this to another human being and not having to carry the burden of this information within his own mind any longer. It occurred to him that he hadn't had this kind of conversation in years and that, for a decade or more, he hadn't had the opportunity to tell someone else how he was feeling or describe the many discomforts and biological idiosyncrasies that play such a persistent role in everyday life.

It was, therefore, quite disheartening when he noticed that Dr. Xie, rather than taking down copious notes on his condition, seemed instead to be struggling with the pace of his description, her eyes twitching from left to right and her hand cocked in a ready position to tap a field on some unseen checklist that corresponded to what he was saying.

He stopped his monologue with a concise summary. "So yes, I have this pain or, kind of like a fullness in my chest. And this morning I coughed up some blood."

"This pain. It happen when eating, correct?" asked Dr. Xie.

"Well, the gurgling happens when I eat. The pain and the cough just come and go, but today it was intense," he said, chiding himself internally for using the word gurgling, which seemed to confuse the doctor.

"So, you say pain happen during the day, but also when eating?" she clarified.

"Yes."

"Do you have a nervous feeling?"

"Yes. The coughing this morning made me nervous."

"Ok. I like to examine you. Is that ok?"

"Yes."

Dr. Xie proceeded with a standard medical examination: pulse, blood pressure, scoping the eyes, ears, and mouth. As she began to palpate his neck and check his breathing, she moved close enough that Randy could sense the warmth radiating from her skin and smell a mixture of perfume and antiseptic soap that, at least in the moment, was surprisingly pleasant. Her hands were smooth and her large, dark eyes were a perfect match for her bright, youthful complexion. She instructed Randy to lay down and asked for permission to lift up his sweater and examine his stomach. As Dr. Xie began moving her hand around his abdomen, Randy felt embarrassed by a small, perceptible shift in his jeans, from which he sought to distance himself by thinking of wiring diagrams for the game room and, when that seemed not to work, the sad, elderly patients he had seen in the waiting room. Dr. Xie, however, was unaware of this mental struggle or its cause, as she pushed firmly on his lower abdomen and checked his face for signs of pain. Although he tried to avoid eye contact at first, he could not help but to look back at her and, rather than struggling to suppress an erotic urge, he instead began to admire the deep human kindness in her eyes and the genuine concern she seemed to have for him in that moment. He was unsure if he had failed to notice this before, or if she was expressing some innate, professional reflex that emerged when caring for patients– an instinct that perhaps she could not express fully in English, but that was powerfully evident in action.

She instructed him to sit up. "Ok. I see no signs of abdomen problems."

"Ok..." he said, waiting for her to continue.

"You say pain happen when eating, and pain happen also at other points of the day. And you say you have a nervous feeling at times, too. I think we start with treating for stress-related acid reflux," she said, pronouncing the Ls in "related" and "reflux" with careful deliberation, "and you maybe come back for follow-up in two weeks. Ok? I prescribe a medication called Protonix. Is for acid. And second medication is Xanax, which helps with stress. Ok? Do you have questions?"

Randy indicated that he understood everything and left with a prescription slip in hand, which he filled at the in-store pharmacy. He noticed that the instructions on his Xanax bottle indicated a frequency of 6 to 12 pills a day as needed for "extreme stress." He let out a mocking chuckle, suspicious at the idea that his lifestyle could produce extreme stress, but happy nonetheless at having such a large quantity of a mild drug.

7

Driving to Scranton was not as easy as it had been in the past, when it was a straight shot on Interstate 81. While Wilkes-Barre and Scranton comprised the eastern frontier of the Energy Corridor and, as such, shared similar economic interests and a common destiny, they had developed an administrative distance over the years, which resulted in the strict monitoring of vehicular traffic entering Scranton. Whereas Wilkes-Barre had integrated itself into the Corridor and became a quasi-hub for a variety of waste storage and disposal operations, Scranton chose not to invite Corridor industry into the city directly, instead preferring to house companies that provided associated services to the energy extraction sector. It did suffer the mass exodus that robbed Wilkes-Barre of much of its pre-Corridor population, but was quick to repurpose many of the abandoned lots and created new office space, shopping centers, and even a golf course. Long-time residents who remained in Scranton lived in the western hills overlooking the city, which were the farthest points from the entrance to the Corridor, while energy industry employees on temporary assignment inhabited the downtown districts and considered the urban setting to be a luxury when compared to the distant settlements within the shale fields. Because of this, the city had a much more modern and inviting appearance, which it tried to maintain by limiting traffic from "industrial" cities and by doing environmental scans on the traffic it did admit— ostensibly to maintain the health and safety of its residents. In practice, however, these procedures were ornamental, as the mega drills of the eastern shale fields were visible from the center of the city, serving as a testament to its inextricable link to the Corridor, and its streets were often so empty that there would be no one to object to the sight of industrial traffic even if it were permitted.

Randy was nonetheless concerned about the scans, because his hauling duties and miles travelled within the fields had certainly left the residue of multiple toxins on his truck. Had he been asked to go to Scranton in the context of any other social request, he would have declined, but he could not resist the intrigue of meeting Blake separately from Jay. He was, of course, cognizant that the trip could very well end in disappointment, just as Jay's big plans from a few weeks ago involved doing a livestream that no one would watch, for a hobby that very few people cared about. He was also very much aware that the reflexive flourish of male sexual fantasy—something that accompanies any one-on-one social outing with a woman—was a hopeless urge that was impossible to fulfill. In fact, Randy had learned long ago that such thoughts intensify in direct proportion to one's sexual and emotional desperation, and thus he ignored them or masturbated to them so that they would pass quickly. Today he could do neither, but he also would not forgive himself if he did not attempt to see her, even if their dinner only amounted to a much-needed break from the monotony of his day-to-day routine.

He sat in the inspection line for about 30 minutes before a drone signaled to him to park his car on a scanner, exit it, and stand in a waiting area. Night was approaching and with it came a burst of arctic air and a thick, cloudy sky that suggested snow. As he watched a wave of translucent red light pass over his Tundra and overheard the driver of an eighteen wheeler arguing with two armed security guards, he became panicked and felt the now familiar gurgling sensation behind his lower-right breast bone, followed by a small splash of metallic-tasting blood on his pallet. He reached into his sweater pocket and shook out an antacid pill and two Xanax, which he struggled to swallow against the grittiness of his mouth and throat. Just as he expected, the drone informed him that his truck had failed the scan but, instead of being turned away, he was instructed to have it decontaminated in a special car wash connected to the security platform. He agreed, paid the $50 decontamination fee, and entered Scranton.

He drove through the empty city and managed to find his way to the campus of the university, which sat on the edge of what used to be the old South Side, a section of Scranton that had since been transformed into an office complex. Though the streets were empty, parking proved quite challenging, as all vehicles within a one-mile radius had to be registered with the campus police. Randy was thus forced to park four miles away and walk along a narrow street, lined with what were the last of the city's abandoned houses, before reaching the clean, bright confines of the university campus. He continued to follow this snaking path through quads of newly built dormitories until he reached a sculpture, which he confirmed to be of Jesus by wiping away a thin layer of snow from its inscription.

It was called "Christ the Teacher" and depicted Jesus stepping down from his cross to beckon to a believer who, perhaps blind, was clutching her heart and gazing into the distance with a countenance frozen at a point between contemplation and rapture. Jesus had an earnest, youthful, and intense expression that contrasted sharply with any depiction Randy could remember of him. His lips were parted and it was unclear if he had inspired or sought to interrupt the reverie of his follower.

Randy stood there for a while and surveyed the campus, worrying that Blake might have intended the text to go to Jay or someone else, which would have been consistent with his luck with women over the years. He looked up at the whitish-purple campus lights, blew out a puff of warm breath with an audible wheeze and watched it float upward and dissipate into the cold night air. He heard voices in the distance and saw the outlines of students walking with their backpacks slung over their shoulders, heading into the library across the mall. It was comforting, he thought, that the rhythms of college life seemed stable in the 16 years since he had graduated, as if this was one of a handful of traditional life experiences that still thrived in and around the Corridor. His nostalgic reflection was interrupted by a playful tap on the shoulder. It was Blake.

"Hey!" she said, her voice tinged both with excitement and surprise.

She was wearing a black Chick-Fil-A uniform that was two-sizes too big and a visor that hid her hair and accentuated the pale white skin and soft curvature of her forehead. Over this she had a peacoat that was a pleasant departure from her usual choice of baggy parkas.

"Hey, what's up?" said Randy, trying to suppress a smile.

"I thought we could have dinner and chill for a bit."

"Good idea. I'm actually in the mood for some Chick-Fil-A," he said, unsure if such an early attempt at dead-pan humor was smart.

She was surprised, but still in possession of the electric smile and bubbly mood with which she greeted him.

"Really?" she asked.

"Nah, wherever you want to go is fine," said Randy.

"I thought we'd go to Organic Gardens...which is just another name for the dining hall. But they have a lot of stuff."

"Cool."

They walked across the campus mall, took a series of left and right turns that Randy found somewhat disorienting, and walked into a large, modern building outfitted with huge panes of glass, freshly-laid red brick, and an intense LED sign that read "Organic Gardens" in green letters. Though the dining hall was sparsely attended, there were at least 20 food counters still ready to serve a variety of meals—from sushi to pizza to organic vegetable soufflés. They even had a dessert bar with homemade waffles and ice cream. Blake handed Randy a guest card and told him to meet her in the back of the dining hall near a row of potted plants. It had occurred to him that he hadn't eaten a hot, fresh meal in months, as only fast food places existed on the hauling routes and he had lost the motivation to cook for himself years ago. He felt drawn to the pizza bar, but instead opted for a steak, a double serving of organic vegetable lasagna and a bottle of Pellegrino. He swiped the guest card at an automated pay station and walked to Blake's table.

"How much do I owe you?" he asked, handing her the card and reaching into his pocket to peel off a few $20s.

"Nothing. Nothing. My treat. Thank you soooo much for coming!" she said, reaching out to squeeze his hand and then retracting her arm, as if upset at transgressing a boundary she had established for herself.

He smiled. "Wow, thank *you*. I don't usually eat like this."

"Enjoy!"

They sat there and began to eat. The food tasted unusually good and Randy enjoyed his first bites of the steak and lasagna with a gusto that had become foreign to him. Unfortunately, however, the ebullience of their first minutes together had faded into a conspicuous silence. He saw that Blake seemed a bit uneasy, alternating between small bites from her noodle bowl and apathetic glances at her phone. He felt his nerves building again, as visions of past awkward social interactions crept into his mind and he feared that, if he didn't say something, the night might devolve into a series of contrived comments that would end in mutual disappointment.

"So did you want to talk to me about something?" he asked, unsure if the question was too direct.

"I mean it's kind of silly. But I wanted to ask you something," she said.

"Sure."

"Fuck, I don't know. I am going to sound really stupid saying this. And, uh..." She paused to let out a nervous laugh. "I asked Jay about this and he thought I was completely nuts."

"It's ok. What is it?"

"I want to join this protest," she said, pausing as if to wait for an indignant reply from Randy.

He smiled.

"It's in Wilkes-Barre and its part of the fight nationwide to raise awareness about the right to clean water...Fuck. I know. I know. I sound stupid. I mean, like, really stupid. Jay pretty much straight up backhanded me when I started talking about this."

"Come on. It's ok. I'm too full to backhand you," said Randy. The joke was awkward in its own right, but also fell flat because he had eaten only half of what was on his plate.

"Ok," said Blake, trying to laugh. "Basically its totally off the grid. Some people from Cincinnati set it up via SkinFlick and we're going to meet at this guy's house. He's like an executive at one of the energy companies and supposedly he pays off the city council to lie about contamination levels in the water supply. And a lot of other companies do this throughout the country. Here."

She typed a code into her phone and handed it to him. He looked down and saw still photos from a porn video.

"You have to, like, scroll through the pictures to see the details," she said, gesturing with her pointer finger.

Randy had heard about SkinFlick but had never really seen it in action. It was a secure messaging app that was inspired by older apps like TextSecure, but worked instead as a vault application. Users of a normal vault app would type a numerical code into a calculator and it would give them access to a hidden folder, which usually contained sexting photos or other types of pornography. In this case, the vault contained images from popular porno websites, but after an arbitrary number of scrolled photos between 2 and 22—called "flicks"—users would see a message from someone who had added their phone number to a messaging database. When they closed the app, the message was deleted and the app would wait to receive the next communication. Messages couldn't be copied or stored outside of the app but, if the senders thought a particular message was important enough, they could aggregate past messages into a larger chain, though this was a practice that was used infrequently by individuals sending messages of questionable legality. If your phone was confiscated, you could give your questioner any code and they would scroll through an endless stream of pictures.

The logic was that it is less harmful to be a deviant than a dissident and, while no app was truly secure, it would at least buy everyone some time before the truth was revealed. The very fact that Blake had this app elevated the seriousness with which Randy perceived her plan. It meant that whatever group she was in contact with was illegal or about to become illegal, and that they trusted her enough to add her number to their database. It was also difficult to find and load an app like SkinFlick in the first place, and probably required a certain degree of aptitude using the dark web. This was something that Jay could do, but, judging by his supposed reaction, it seemed unlikely that he would have helped her install the software.

He scrolled through a few more pics until he came to the message, which appeared as a black screen with dim white letters and included, after he scrolled down far enough, a screen capture of a Google map and directions to a house on Mercedes Drive—a street in a secluded residential neighborhood on the banks of the Susquehanna River that was said to be the last place in Wilkes-Barre that people voluntarily chose to live. The mayor, several city officials, and some mid-level employees of Geo Services Corp. and Independence Energy were rumored to reside there, and the neighborhood allegedly had a secure perimeter and round the clock surveillance. The message stated that the man who lived at the address in question was responsible for paying off city officials to fake the city's water contamination report on behalf of Geo Services Corp., and that the actual levels of contamination from stored fracking waste and the other industrial waste products processed and stored in the city were 8 times the reported findings. Under a section called "Plan of Action," the message instructed protestors to wear black skull and cross bone shirts and bring a water bottle filled with either Wilkes-Barre tap water or water from the Susquehanna River to dump on the man's lawn. It ended with the following lines: "Now we hit them where they live. Take no prisoners!"

Randy could understand why Jay was upset, as involvement in this kind of activity constituted a line which, once crossed, meant that there was no turning back. In the Corridor, people who protested were met with severe reprisals from police and the local security forces, especially after an incident in 2022 when a group of angry activists planted a bomb in a benzene storage facility in the shale fields and were subsequently labeled as terrorists. Since then, polite inquiry at city council meetings was the furthest extent of protest that was tolerated in Wilkes-Barre. While Randy and Jay did operate in a legal gray area at times, it was one that could be managed and therefore treated as a calculated risk. Direct opposition was very much a different beast and had a totally different set of rules. Whereas cities like New York tolerated civil disobedience as evidence of its progressive heritage, the shale fields functioned under the imperatives of economic expansion and technological development, which allowed for no interruptions and no insubordination. The understanding—among the corporations that owned the fields and the residents of the cities that existed in and around them—was that if you chose to stay, you accepted the reality of your circumstances and did not interfere.

Randy stared at the message longer than he needed to, hoping to formulate some response that would respect her convictions but convince her not to participate in the protest. He couldn't stand the thought of Blake, at twenty years old, walking into a situation that could result in a long period of incarceration or something worse. And yet, when he glanced up at her and saw the expectant seriousness in her eyes, as if she firmly believed that he would understand and sympathize with her position, he decided to buy some time and delay the paternalistic admonishments that were swirling in his head.

"I didn't know you were into this kind of thing," he said as he handed the phone back to her.

"I had a class on it last year and I did some reading and it's so fucked up, what's going on. I think people are dying because of this and we don't hear anything about it in the news. People just need to get off their asses and *do* something. Don't you think?"

Randy was again unsure of how to respond. A life at the edge of the Corridor meant that statements of belief, rooted in social consciousness and unequivocal in intent, were rare and not worthy of serious consideration. He and most others whom he knew functioned in a constant state of pragmatic pessimism, in which everyone expected the worst possible outcomes to their actions and tried to prepare for them and manage them intelligently, to the extent that this was possible. When some instance of personal or communal doom did crop up, it was written off as the way of things and not given all that much thought. Survival in the Corridor meant, to a large extent, that people had to navigate two realities: the world of spoken interaction, which offered reasonable explanations or artful deflections and diversions from the deteriorating political and economic order– and the world of personal action in which, consciously or unconsciously, people adapted to their circumstances and sought to maximize their dwindling opportunities for security and comfort. This mindset, combined with the digital escapism that his game room provided, allowed Randy to evade the larger questions of environmental and economic justice that lingered in the background of his life.

He decided to lie. "Totally. It is totally fucked up."

"And, I don't know," she continued, "You've lived in the city your whole life and I think your voice would make a difference in this protest. We want to get as many actual residents out there as possible, so I figured I'd see if you wanted to join us."

Randy felt a lump form in his throat. He had initially assumed that she was just asking for his advice, but didn't think that she would invite him to become directly involved in the protest. He would never put himself at this kind of risk and had spent his whole life minimizing his exposure to the security infrastructure of the region, at least outside of what was necessary for his job. This was a direct call to action for which he was not prepared.

Blake sensed his hesitation.

"I know," she said. "I told you. It's so fucking stupid, but I just can't let it go for some reason. I just want to do something; you know? We sit here in class and get all of this info and stuff, and then when the hour's over we just focus on homework or finding internships or jobs in other cities. And we can make a difference right here, but we choose not to. Kind of makes you sick after a while."

"No, I hear you," said Randy, kicking himself for not putting an immediate end to this idea. "It's just that, sometimes it is hard to know what to do. You know, to fight it. I guess people just have to get organized."

"Yeah," said Blake, "and these guys from Cincinnati are super organized. They've got this guy who works the security gates to the development on board and they said that they're going to get some international media coverage. Like have reporters there somehow."

"Do they know anything about how dangerous it could be?" asked Randy.

"Ummm, they said it's a risk, but that they have a record of non-violent actions and that if the police know we have the press there, they won't react too harshly."

Randy knew that she didn't quite believe what she had said, but he continued playing along.

"That's true," he said. "They won't make it a total shit show if they think people will see it online."

"Yeah, totally. And I'm just tired of sitting around at school or cleaning tables at work wondering when I can be a part of something important. I might be destined to just rot here, but I don't want to do it in silence. I just wanna have a voice. At least once."

Randy looked into her eyes and saw that her conviction was unwavering, but he couldn't help thinking that it was motivated by a youthful naiveté which led her to believe that her actions at this protest could change the political direction of the city. He again sought to delay offering his participation by asking another question.

"Did you ever think of getting out of here after graduation? You could join the environmentalist movement in New York or San Francisco or something. You could do grad school somewhere else and fight this thing on the national stage. That might work even better."

She looked disappointed. "My parents scraped together enough money for tuition so that I could go here, but I've had to take out serious loans to pay for room and board and I'll be working for-fucking-ever just to pay them back. Plus, I've got Jay so, let's face it, I'm never getting the fuck out of here."

"That's not true," said Randy, "You're not even twenty-one. You don't know what the future holds. It's too early to say that you're never leaving. Never say never." He cringed at the clichéd advice he had just offered.

"No, it's true," Blake replied, "You know it's true. You've lived here long enough to know it's true. Let's face it, college isn't a springboard to anything. It's like the last stop for me, my last chance at being even somewhat independent. My parents didn't get out of here. Jay isn't going anywhere. And I'm stuck here. And I hate myself for being too fucking scared to just go to this thing alone. It's fucked up, but that's why I'm asking. I thought you'd say yes. I mean, you live here too and it should matter to you, but I understand if it doesn't."

Randy was surprised and refreshed by her candor. She had the courage to confront the reality of a pervasive corruption that he had encountered for the majority of his adult life but chose not to name. The sadness and vulnerability that seemed to lurk just beneath the surface of her personality had manifested itself in reddened, tearful eyes and a look of disgust that she tried to hide by staring into the distance.

"Look," Randy said with hesitancy in his voice, "I didn't say that I wasn't going. It's just...Oh fuck, I just care about you and so I was just saying what I thought...I mean, I don't really even know you that well, but I just don't want you to get hurt and this shit seems serious. Like, really serious. But you're right. I should care. I should have cared my whole life, but I did nothing and just fucking sat around. So yeah, I'll go."

"I understand that you probably think I'm crazy," Blake said, "so I get it if you just want to think about it and get back to me."

Randy reached out and placed his hand over the top of hers. She laughed and stared down at her tray.

"Hey," said Randy, squeezing her hand as she tried to pull back from his grip. "Hey, look at me. I'm going. You're right. You're right about everything. I should have cared about this shit years ago, but I chose not to. Maybe if I had done something, been a part of something back then, things wouldn't have gone to hell so quickly. Or, at the very least, I could say that I actually fought for something. Sounds a lot better than saying that I sat in a garage while my fellow citizens were being poisoned."

"Ok. Ok....Cool," she said, her hesitation and nervousness subsiding. "Well, it's this Saturday so, um, I'll just text you when I know the time. I won't say the exact time but I'll ask a video game question or something and then you can show up like an hour later. Does that work?

"Yeah. Fine."

As they bussed their trays and exited the cafeteria, Randy found himself caught up in a state of aggressive self-reproach. The cautious hermit in him was furious that he agreed to put himself at risk just because a girl asked him to do so and, at some deeper level of his humanity, he was angry with himself for lacking the boldness and courage that Blake possessed. Whereas she was compelled to do something that had deep personal meaning in spite of the risk that it posed, he had done nothing to realize the modest dreams of his youth and never felt compelled to go beyond himself for any person or cause. While Blake was disturbed by the contradiction that existed between her life as a student and the environmental realities of life in the Corridor, Randy had been content to delay and defer even the slightest recognition of such contradictions until he was too old and too complacent to make any significant changes to his life. Walking out of the dining hall and into the now snowy campus mall, he wondered why, in view of his obvious personal inadequacies, she ever felt the need to confide in him and include him in this plan. There were surely any number of idealistic, motivated people on this campus with a drive and potential that dwarfed his own, and yet she made this request of him. He was tempted to ask her about this, but decided against it, for fear it would sound like he was backing out.

When they returned to the statue where they had met, Blake turned to him and, grabbing his hands, asked, "Why don't you come back to my place for a bit?"

"Yeah, sure," said Randy, surprised by the request, "but I thought Jay said you couldn't have guests for the night?"

She giggled. "Who said you were staying the night?"

Randy was embarrassed that his mind made the instantaneous connection between her request and an invitation to stay the night. There was, he supposed, a certain degree of innate male egotism or a cultural reflex that clouded the mind with the belief that such connections were possible and followed logically from the offer to "come back to my place," but as he looked down at the Zelda sweater that covered his paunch and his tattered jeans and Converse sneakers, it became clear that he was not a romantic option for her. It was more likely that he was confusing an emergent platonic relationship with some background sexual tension that always existed in his mind. Or, as a former girlfriend told him years ago, he was the kind of guy who confused attraction with the "friend zone," a sort of relationship gray area that had the trappings of emotional intimacy without any kind of sexual desire on the part of the woman.

"Oh, no, I didn't mean it that way," he said with embarrassment, "I just thought you couldn't have visitors at all."

"No, visitors are cool," she said with a smile.

Randy followed her to one of the new student dorms on a quad at the far end of the campus. They stepped into the elevator and took it to the fourth floor it in an anticipatory, uncomfortable silence; exiting to find a group of students sitting in a large, luxurious lounge area with a fireplace in the center of the room and OLED TV display strips on the walls and ceiling. This piqued Randy's tech enthusiast curiosity, though his urge to examine them was outweighed by his fear of being acknowledged as an outsider. The students looked up at them as they passed, but seemed not to notice or care that Randy was visibly older than they were.

Blake's room was located in a long hallway next to a window that looked out onto the city. When they entered, Randy was surprised to see that it was a spacious, single-person room that looked more like a hotel room than a student accommodation. She had a queen-sized bed in a small alcove and a desk placed in front of a large bay window. There was a couch on the wall to the left of the alcove and a large TV/entertainment center across from it. The room was so clean and pleasant that he felt embarrassed that she had visited his run down house and game room.

"Look," she said, handing him a slip of paper with a code on it, "We have free Internet here. Why don't you surf around a bit? I kind of smell like fried chicken and French fry grease, so I'm going to hop in the shower. I won't be too long."

Randy was again surprised and unsettled by the fact that she wanted to shower. He didn't even know why she wanted him to come back with her in the first place and, if there was no romantic intention on her part, why did it matter that she smelled like French fry grease? He thought perhaps that he had misread her for the entire evening, that she was expecting something from him of which he had no insight and for which he had not prepared. He lamented the fact that his social skills had eroded over the years, to the point that he couldn't read whatever subtle cues she was sending him and wondered if perhaps he was too old to understand how flirting or hook-ups worked these days. He also couldn't shake the feeling that what he was doing was scandalous, but wasn't sure if the scandal was that he went home with a girl eighteen years his junior or if the true scandal was that he had made so little progress in life that his presence in a dorm seemed completely innocuous.

The stress of these thoughts made him feel nauseous, to the point that the pain in his chest began to intensify and grow into the kind of gurgling that had accompanied his attack this morning. He felt like gasping for air but, as he could hear that Blake had turned off the water to the shower and was drying herself, he tried to suppress his urge to gasp and cough. He could feel a strong, secondary pressure move upward through his chest and deposit a small amount of regurgitated lasagna in his mouth, which had a strong taste of garlic and blood. He forced it back down and panicked. He felt as if some cynical, cosmic force was causing his body to rebel against him right at the moment when he could, for the first time in years, have an emotional or physical connection with a girl for whom he cared. He sprang up, looked around the room, and eventually noticed a stack of water bottles on the floor near Blake's bed. He grabbed one, rummaged around for the Xanax in his pocket, swallowed two pills with the whole bottle, and hoped that it would wash away the taste of the noxious mound of undigested food that had just been in his mouth. He continued to search the room for some gum or mints, but could find none, so he sat down and decided to try some meditative breathing techniques as he surfed the Internet, which was gloriously fast.

Blake exited the bathroom a few minutes later, dressed in baggy pajama pants and an oversized University of Scranton t-shirt, which draped down to her knees and revealed the faint outline of her breasts. Her hair, no longer in a tight knot, touched her shoulders and seemed to have a cherry-colored hue that Randy had not noticed before. Her feet were bare and her toenails were painted black, which matched her black finger nails and reminded him of the so-called goth girls he had admired in high school. She noticed the bottle of Xanax still resting in his lap and snatched it before he could react.

"What's this stuff?" she asked with enthusiastic curiosity.

"Oh, nothing. Just this medicine that I have to take every now and then.

"Xanax. Cool. This gives you a nice, mellow high. Mind if I have some?"

Randy was surprised but agreed. She swallowed a pill, grabbed a water bottle for herself, and sat down next to him on the couch in a lotus position.

"Thanks for coming back here," she said, with her hands in her lap, picking at her nails.

"Sure," said Randy, not knowing what else to say.

"Look, I know that the protest is going to be dangerous. And I know that you aren't the type of guy who usually sticks his neck out like this. Jay tells me your life was kind of fucked up and that you're pretty apolitical. But I just want you to know that I'll take the blame. I mean, you can say that you didn't know what would happen and that I had the app or whatever. It just means a lot that you'll be there. For me and the movement."

Randy was a bit perplexed. He found it amusing that Jay felt he possessed the capacity to even differentiate political from apolitical dispositions, and he didn't recall telling him about his past. He was also ashamed that Blake felt the need to convince him that things would be ok and that she would protect him. Though he never thought of himself in terms of concepts like manhood and masculine pride, he felt compelled to defend himself.

"Look," he said, making eye contact with her, "I know I'm a burnout pushing 40. I know that I could have left this city years ago or stayed and fought against the bullshit, but instead I sat on my ass doing jack shit. So let's be honest, you've got more to live for than I do and if something happens, it's me that will take the blame. I'm gonna protect you at this thing."

"I don't think you're a burnout," she said, resting her hand on his shoulder and rubbing his arm. "I think you're a guy who forgot what it means to have some hope. And I'm not saying that in an insulting way. I mean, you have all this knowledge, but you just don't do anything with it. That's why I want you to do this game stream thing. Share that knowledge with people. Teach people about all this cool stuff. It might seem trivial, but you'll have a voice. Same with the protest. You'll be there when we send this message to the country. The media will be there. It could be the beginning of something and you'll be part of it."

Randy appreciated her kindness, but knew that she had a vision of him that was not completely accurate.

"Thanks for saying that," he said, "but I'm nothing special. I mean, look at where I live, look at this city, I don't think the kind of hope exists for me that exists for you. I want to help you. And I will help you. But I don't think anyone is going to care about this gaming night or will even know that I am from Wilkes-Barre at the protest. I'm kind of an invisible guy in so many ways."

"Now you are starting to sound like an old man," she said, punching him in the arm and smiling. "You'll know that you went and that you took a stand against this injustice. And the gaming night, I mean, shit. People will watch what you do and discover this whole era of art and creativity that's been kind of forgotten. That means something."

"I don't really see my collection as being art or myself as being all that inspirational," he replied.

"See, that's where you're wrong. Take Jay. He's, like, a typical guy. He does his programming and his tech stuff and worries about his different gigs, but he doesn't think much about anything else. But when he met you and you were nice to him and introduced him to this forgotten culture, he changed. He was really excited by all of it. You could do that for a lot of people."

"But there is a ton of stuff like that out there already," Randy said. "It's not exactly hidden. I mean, googling video games will bring up decades of coverage on gaming."

"Yeah," she said with a sigh, "but you know how the Internet is. If it isn't new, people just assume it doesn't exist. Plus, even if no one sees it, there is power and meaning in just expressing yourself."

She stood up, grabbed a tablet sitting on her desk and sat back down next to Randy, this time resting her head on his shoulder and pressing her body against his.

"I want to show this to you," she said, calling up an online drop box with some video files in it. "I do film production as a minor and I made some super short films about the area and posted them online. That's how I found those guys in Cincinnati. I want you to watch this one."

She played a video file entitled "Is This Our World?" It began with a sequence of shots from a car driving along one of the public highways on the outskirts of the Corridor, panning from the traffic lines, to the edge of the highway, to the drill sites on the horizon. The film then cut to shots of abandoned houses in downtown Wilkes-Barre, and concluded with a time-lapse shot of the shale fields from above, perhaps from atop the Endless Mountains to the north of the city. The height and the choice of camera perspectives made the fields look like a single, massive alien spacecraft as they began to illuminate at sunset. Throughout this last sequence, the film again made quick jump cuts, this time to the lines of a poem, which read:

> "This World is Not Conclusion
> A Species Stands Beyond-
> Invisible as Music-
> But Positive as Sound- "

Randy could feel a tear swell in the corner of his eye. The video had a strange beauty to it, even though it was technically and thematically simplistic and very much the work of an amateur. If he had encountered it on the Internet, he would have probably clicked away, but being forced to watch it, in these circumstances, with all that he knew about Blake, led to a torrent of intense emotion that he struggled to contain. These two minutes of footage seemed to signify the tragedy of his life: the depravation of his surroundings, the contradiction of his job, and the existence within him of a deep cynicism that had prevented him from ever having the purity of vision and clarity of purpose to synthesize and express what Blake had woven into this film.

Noticing the emotion on Randy's face, Blake leaned over and kissed him, first on the cheek, and then on the lips. He froze in an effort to regain his emotional composure and process what was happening. He worried again about the state of his breath and, opening his lips to allow her tongue to slide into contact with his, hoped that she could not taste the blood that had been in his mouth. Knowing that a line had been crossed and confident that he did not want to turn back, he reached his right hand around her and rested it on the waistband of her jogging pants, allowing his fingers to dip ever so slightly toward her bottom. She then threw her leg over his lap and began kissing him with increasing aggression. He could feel the dry ridges of her chapped lips against his, which proved to be an incredible turn on, and sensed his erection pressing up through his jeans to make contact with her inner thigh. He then mustered the courage to put both hands on her hips as she got up on her knees, pressed her pelvis into his chest, and leaned down to kiss him from above. When he moved his hand behind her shirt and began to trace the ridge of her back with his finger, she collapsed back down again, hugging him and resting her head on his shoulder.

"I can't do this," she said, trying to catch her breath.

Randy was silent, but slowly moved his hands away from her body and rested them at his side.

"I'm so, so sorry." she continued, "I really care about you and if...if this continues I'm gonna want you to stay, and if you stay things are gonna get really complicated and I don't know if I can take that."

She rolled off of him and curled up into a ball on the other end of the couch. Randy stood up and felt light-headed.

"It's ok. It's ok. I'll do whatever you want," he said.

"You've made me so happy tonight, really" she replied, "I just can't do this to Jay."

"No. I understand," said Randy, reaching for his Xanax and smartphone, which had wedged themselves into the back of the couch. "So, I'll go then?"

He hoped she would reconsider. She didn't answer, but stood up and kissed him again.

"Thank you so much, for everything," she said. "If things were different..."

Randy drifted backwards toward the door. Blake stood there, wiping tears from her cheeks and offering some soft, uncomfortable laughter. As Randy reached for the doorknob, she gave him an awkward smile and a slight shrug of her shoulders, a gesture which he struggled to interpret. Did she want him to remain in the room or was the shrug of her shoulders a physical manifestation of her desire for things to be different, while simultaneously acknowledging this desire as an impossibility? He walked out into the hallway, closed the door behind him, and waited for a while, hoping that, if she did want him to come back, she would give him a sign.

He heard nothing.

He exited the building and felt the immediate sting of the wintry night on his cheeks, which were still moist with a mixture of their tears. The snow had continued throughout his stay and was falling with increasing intensity, covering the campus in a silent cloak of white powder. He checked his phone. 2:00am. He walked alone, across the campus, through the rows of abandoned houses, back to his car.

8

"Dude, they're not gonna have it," said Randy, bouncing on his tip-toes to get a better view of a line of people trying to enter a high school gymnasium.

"Chill, man," said Jay, "the post said TurboGrafx and Turbo Duo.

"Yeah, that was either bait to get you to show up or it just means they have games for those systems," said Randy, irritated and checking the time on his phone. "We shouldn't have even come here."

"It's a gaming convention, dude," said Jay, "the only one on the fuckin' East Coast. If anyone is gonna have this system, it's these guys."

Gaming conventions, a popular staple of the retro culture of Randy's youth, had died out after hitting the peak of their popularity in the early 2020s, when events like San Diego Comic Con were still drawing hundreds of thousands of guests and getting mainstream media coverage for their lavish staging and over-the-top cosplay. As the general public became unable to pay the escalating ticket prices of the major shows and casual interest in video games, anime, and sci-fi began to wane, convention culture was left in the hands of small, dedicated fanbases who fought to find appropriate venues and gather enough online interest to stage the events and keep the convention spirit alive. At first, the result in the retro video game community was a massive consolidation of conventions into regional events, which were staged in major cities throughout the country and were better attended than the sum total of the smaller shows that they replaced. Eventually, however, floor space became too expensive and attendance dwindled to the point that these shows became unsustainable. The major organizers, however, were unwilling to admit defeat and instead scaled down their gatherings to fill smaller or nontraditional venues such as flea-market lots, churches, and public libraries.

In this case, the convention—called the East Coast Gaming Mega Show, a spiritual successor of sorts to the once popular *Too Many Games* convention— was taking place in a high school gymnasium in Allentown, Pennsylvania. The school was located in a residential neighborhood about an hour south of Wilkes-Barre and, though it was a modest setting, it offered the convention organizers and attendees a few key advantages. Having incurred significant damage in a hurricane five years ago and unable to use about half of its classrooms, the school was eager to monetize the functional space it had left in an effort to raise enough money for repairs. Their fee was reasonable, their parking was ample, and they asked very few questions about the nature of the event and didn't demand a cut of the take from each individual dealer, as some hosts did. As a result, the convention became a yearly event on the school's growing calendar of building rentals and still managed to draw a reasonable crowd by the standards of the day, even if it was a shell of its former self.

Randy was never a fan of conventions as such, but always felt compelled to go to them while he was amassing the bulk of his collection. In his twenties, if a show was on the east coast, he would attend it without fail, spending days on the road and sleeping in his car, all in the hopes of finding a rare score. At 27, he even saved up enough money to travel to Portland, Oregon to attend the famous *Portland Retro Gaming Expo*, where he blew two months' salary on *Crusaders of Centy* for the Sega Genesis and *Hexyz Force* for the PSP. His devotion to the convention scene bordered on the religious in these early days, not so much because the experiences themselves were epiphanic or revelatory, but because his trips were—in the context of first-world, obsessive fandom— grueling pilgrimages on which he sacrificed personal comfort and safety for the sake of finding and holding the sacred artifacts of his chosen hobby. He had camped out on the streets of Chicago for early bird access to a pre-NES era hardware convention, ate Ramen for a month to purchase *Earthbound* at a show on Staten Island, and even hitch-hiked on the DC Beltway when his car broke down on the way to *Anime Expo*.

And yet, despite the zeal of consumption that drove him to attend these events, Randy did not care for the experience of actually being in the convention crowds once he arrived. Contrary to the popular belief that these gatherings were opportunities for like-minded people to come together and have fun, he always felt uneasy and depressed when standing in throngs of people who, dressed-up in faux-vintage t-shirts and game character cosplay, engulfed him as he perused the show floors in search of his nostalgic treasures. In the mid-2010s, when he started attending, there was even a certain enthusiastic staging of what had become a standardized retro personality, in which a mass of people celebrated the same games, shared in the same ironic sense of humor, and put their own, supposedly personal spins on the then popular hipster aesthetic. As the years went on, however, this attitude faded into a kind of desperate compulsion, with people silently flipping through boxes of old games to search out the last vestiges of a dying hobby, as if driven by an internalized sunken cost fallacy. To Randy, what was advertised as a community was, in actuality, little more than communal anti-social behavior—a group of people sharing the same physical space while engaging in what were ultimately insular pursuits.

Even in 2030, on the outskirts of the Corridor, in a dilapidated building, little had changed. Though the gymnasium looked half empty from a distance, Randy and Jay were forced to wait in the obligatory, massive line of fatigued fans who smelled of sweat and onions– a reality that was more excusable considering the present day economic desperation, but was sadly an olfactory holdover from conventions held in times of relative ease and prosperity. Despite the fact that the vendors at the show were few in number and there were no panels or live music advertised, the ticket prices were still holding at $100, which was the accepted cost of a major show in New York or San Francisco in the heyday of the convention. The line moved at a glacial pace and, to Randy's surprise, the entrance fee was swipe-to-pay only, which was a major problem, as he had not updated his smartphone cash account in months and didn't have a modern enough SIM card to make a secure cash transfer over the mobile Internet. Jay covered for him, however, and they entered the show.

The handful of vendors that did attend sat along the edges of the room in a U shape, while the center of the show floor was filled with handmade, colorful particle board carvings in the shape of famous video game characters–a lively and heartfelt touch to a room that was otherwise littered with old bookshelves, desks, digital whiteboards and had a musky odor emanating from its leaking roof and rotted, green basketball floor. The guests seemed sullen and walked around without puprose, occasionally checking prices on their smartphones or smirking when they encountered a game or accessory that was familiar or meaningful. The only exception was a cheerful young girl, dressed in a Samus Aran costume, who hopped through the maze of particleboard carvings and pretended to zap the characters with her blaster arm. She seemed not to have a care in the world, as if she derived as much pleasure from the simple acts of running and hopping as she did from wearing her elaborately constructed space suit. Randy stared at her for a while, wondering if she knew anything about the character she was portraying and questioning how she was able to make or buy a costume that was so brilliantly designed. She stopped in front of him and began spinning around in circles, her frizzy black hair swaying back and forth and the lights on her outfit blinking in rhythm with her movements. She jumped to face him, pointed her blaster arm at him and, with an innocent, giggly smile, began making laser sounds before she ran back through the maze.

"Ok dude," said Jay, "let's stake out that Turbo Duo."

"I'm telling you, man. No one brought a Duo to a show like this," said Randy.

"Bro, we drove all the way out here, so we better look. Fuck's a matter with you anyway? You used to be all about the hunt!"

"Fine."

Unlike in the past, the vendors did not have signage indicating who they were and what they were selling. They sat at long, gray folding tables on which they placed their modest inventories and hoped for a sale. As independent video game stores had long since died out, the vendors here were a mix of big collectors paring down their holdings, former store owners selling off old stock, and a few of the remaining Internet personalities who still felt compelled to work the convention circuit and sell their books and DVDs. The vendors shared the same disposition as the attendees, glancing halfheartedly at their smartphone screens and ignoring the people circulating in front of them, unless conversation was initiated by a potential customer.

"Excuse me," said Jay, trying to get the attention of a vendor at one of the first tables on the left-hand side of the room. "Do you carry Turbo Duos?"

The man, dressed in a graying undershirt and a John Deere hat, looked up at Jay in weary disbelief. "Fuck off, kid."

The next few tables specialized in pressed bead art and other handmade video game trinkets and were devoid of foot traffic. One man claimed to be the woodworker who made the particleboard maze and inquired, in a desperate tone, if Randy or Jay would like to commission a statue for their front lawns. They declined.

As Jay wandered away in search of the Duo, Randy noticed what he thought was an old online acquaintance sitting at a table in the far corner of the room. Though the man had aged and had gained a significant amount of weight, he had the familiar high cheekbones and curly-blond hair of a YouTuber named The Unnecessary Gamer—a gaming comic that had risen to popularity in the late 2010s with a series of online skits in which he played different video game characters getting drunk in a bar. He had also written a few video game guidebooks for collectors and took to the convention circuit doing a stand-up act of his impersonations and selling his books after his set.

"Bill?" said Randy, walking over to the table and extending his hand.

The man looked up and, while it seemed that he did not recognize Randy specifically, he smiled as if he were relieved that someone was talking to him. He stood up to shake Randy's hand and, in the process, his worn Final Fantasy VII pre-order bonus t-shirt scrunched upward towards his chest, revealing his huge, scarred gut, which jiggled with the motion of the handshake. He then returned to his seat and began rummaging through a gym bag on the table, eventually locating a gray electrolarynx, which he jabbed under his chin and began speaking.

"Nice to see you," he said in a high-pitched, robotic voice. "What can I do for you?"

"Uh, Bill," said Randy, taken aback by his appearance and the sound of the voice synthesizer, "I, uh, I'm not sure if you remember me. Randy from Wilkes-Barre. We skyped a few times; like, ten years ago–and you helped me locate that copy of *Valkyrie Profile*. Just, uh, wanted to say hi."

"Oh, yeah. I remember." said Bill. "Glad I could help out."

"Really? That's awesome."

"Nah, I'm just fuckin' with you. I have no idea who ya are," said Bill, breaking out in a metallic laugh.

"Oh, well, I guess you're a busy guy. I thought you lived in L.A. though. Why're you out here for this show? Seems like a bit of a trek."

"Wow, you know me real well! You have a premium sub to my channel or something?"

"No, like I said, we talked a few times and I read a couple of your guidebooks back in the day."

"Now, that's awesome," said Bill, wiping away the sweat from under his chin and repositioning the electrolarynx. "I got a new one coming out. 'The Unnecessary Gamer's Guide to the Nintendo 3DS.' It's a really cool book. Here, I can sell you a download code for $15."

"No, that's ok," said Randy, "I really just wanted to say hello and catch up. See how you're doing."

"Then why not do me a favor and buy something, bro?" asked Bill, straining to increase the volume of his synthesized voice. "Look, I got Volumes 1 and 2 of 'Pixels in a Bar' on UHD Blu-Ray. I can sell'em both to you for $40. Come on, the price is only good for convention weekend."

"Look, man," said Randy, "I really liked that series and watched them all, seriously, I was just trying to chat for a bit. I'm really not interested in buying anything off of you."

"Ok, how about this. Give me a buck and I'll sing the theme song to the Super Mario Bros. cartoon. Come on, dude. 'Swing your arms from side to side.' You know, come on, that'd be cool, right?"

Randy hesitated. "Uh, I'm not sure if..."

"Dude, come on," said Bill, standing up and gesturing to the other vendors, "it'll be rad. 'Swing your arms from side to side.' Who wants to hear it?"

At this point Jay pushed his way through the small crowd that had gathered in front of Bill's table in curiosity. He told Randy that he found the vendor selling the Turbo Duo and tried to pull him away from Bill's aggressive spectacle, but it was to no avail, as Bill started cursing at them and accusing them of wasting his time.

"Dude," said Jay, "just chill. What do you want from us?"

"Dude," Bill said, "just chill and give me a buck and I'll sing a sweet-ass song. What's wrong with that? It'd be fucking hilarious!"

"Whatever, man," said Jay, reaching into his pocket and throwing a dollar down in front of Bill, "just do it already."

Bill pawed at the dollar and shoved it into his pocket, leaving a small puddle of sweat on the table. He then stood up and began an enthusiastic rendition of the theme song to the 1989 *Super Mario Bros. Super Show* cartoon series, alternating between its actual lyrics and chiptune sounds he made by humming into his voice synthesizer. Some in the crowd tried to initiate a chorus of claps, which by now had become a near reflexive response to any public attempt at singing or dancing—only here the rhythm of the applause was rather apathetic and uncoordinated. Despite this, Bill was inspired enough to start making up his own, somewhat sexual lyrics to the song, and doing a poor approximation of the moonwalk dance around his table.

Randy and Jay snuck away during the performance and made their way across the room, joining the end of a large line of people in front of one of the few tables that actually had a large inventory of games.

"That dude was fuckin' crazy," said Jay.

"Yeah, totally," said Randy, again raising himself on his tip-toes to assess the line.

"This lady's got the goods, man," said Jay.

"So you saw an actual Turbo Duo on her table?"

"Not exactly, bro. But she's got the signs for it."

"That doesn't mean shit," said Randy.

"Just wait and see. I'm feeling lucky."

Randy ignored the comment and again tried to survey the line, this time flanking it to get a closer look at the table and determine why it wasn't moving.

"There's always a fucking line at these things," he said, returning to stand next to Jay.

"Nothin' you can do, bro" said Jay.

"I can fuckin' leave," said Randy.

"Dude, we're almost there. Just wait."

"Whatever."

"Look, I got a funny story actually," said Jay.

"Yeah, what is it?"

"Get this. Blake comes to me the other day and is like 'I wanna do this protest in Wilkes-Barre.' And I'm like, 'You're outta your fuckin' mind, bitch.' And she fucking insisted and shit and we had this big fight. You believe that?

Randy felt his chest seize up at the mention of the protest. He assumed that Blake hadn't told Jay of their meeting or the fact that he agreed to go with her but, as he wasn't fully sure, he decided to play it safe.

"Protest?" asked Randy, "People aren't dumb enough to do that around here."

"I know, dude," he said. "And it wasn't even about women's' lib or that shit. She wants to, like, protest about the water or something. I'm like, drink out of a fucking bottle if it bothers you. Why get arrested over it?"

"That's insane," said Randy, observing Jay out of the corner of his eye.

The line moved.

"But she was so fuckin' serious. I've never seen her like that. I mean, she totally lost it on me."

"Well, you do crazy things when you're young," said Randy, now confident that measured, clichéd responses would get him through the conversation.

"Yeah, well, you know what I heard? One of my sources told me that there was this guy who made these threats at a town hall meeting or something. And they arrested him and fuckin' water-boarded him in the basement of the municipal building. Just like in the fuckin' Iraq War."

"Now, come on, that shit doesn't happen at town hall meetings. The old-timers at those meetings just complain about the flowers in the park and stuff. No one is getting water-boarded there."

The line inched forward again.

"I'm serious, dude," said Jay, poking Randy in the shoulder, "my source said he was like part of some militia."

"Whatever, man," said Randy, "I don't think there are enough guys in Wilkes-Barre sober enough to form a real militia."

"Well, you don't have to believe it if you don't want to, but it's true."

"And who's your source on this one?" asked Randy. "The guy who sells you your weed or the guy who gives you those fuckin' lollipops."

"Ha. Funny dude," said Jay, "but seriously though, I'm not lettin' her go. I'm not lettin' her get dragged off into some basement like that. I'll fuckin' tie her up if I have to. I'm not losing my girl because of some bleeding-heart liberal nonsense fuckin' protest."

"She's probably not serious. She could just be using this as an excuse to be mad at you for something else," said Randy, repressing feelings of guilt. He knew that Jay was right, regardless of the inarticulate manner in which he stated his reasons. The protest was a serious threat not only to Jay and Blake's relationship, but to Blake's very life, and he felt strengthened in his resolve to protect her, even if it meant that he would have to take the brunt of whatever police aggression might occur on the scene.

"I hope you're right, man" said Jay.

They finally reached the front of the line and were greeted by a snarky, four-hundred-pound woman dressed in a full-body Pikachu outfit. In front of her was an impressive spread of 16 and 32-bit era games, including some rare and expensive items that seemed unfit for the setting, such as a mint, limited edition copy of *Lunar 2* on the Playstation and an unopened copy of *E.V.O.: Search for Eden* on the Super Nintendo, which alone would have brought in several thousand dollars at the height of the collecting boom. In addition to these gems, she did indeed have a sizable collection of TurboGrafx and Turbo Duo games and accessories, including a *Super Air Zonk* for the Turbo Duo Super CD that activated Randy's collecting instinct, despite not owning a system on which to play it.

"So which one of you guys is taking the front and which one is taking the back?" said the woman.

"Huh?" said Jay.

"Of the table, as in, browsing. Cause sweetheart, your Pokeballs aren't big enough to catch me."

Jay still seemed confused at the innuendo, likely because he had never seen or played a Pokémon game before.

"Look," said Jay, with slight hesitation, "my friend here is looking for a Turbo Duo and we saw that you have some games and controllers for it, so we wanted to know if you got one for sale."

"Yeah," said the woman, "and I'm looking for a cure for divorce and Krispy Kremes. Doesn't mean I can just walk around and find it."

"We didn't expect you to have one at the show," interjected Randy, "but it's unusual for someone to be selling games for it in quantity these days. We figured you might have a line on one or know someone who does."

"I might," said the woman, leaning forward and resting her chin on her Pikachu mitts, "but, what're you prepared to do for it?"

"I would be prepared to pay money for it or do a trade," said Randy with a smirk.

"I'm afraid that's not good enough," she said. "The way I see it, you gotta be willing to hunt around in the tall grass before that system'll appear."

"Uh, yeah" said Randy, "look, I can give you my number and if a system pops up and it isn't the price of a Ferrari, you can call me."

"See ladies," she said to another group of vendors as she entered Randy's number into her phone, "you guys told me to wear the Mai Shiranui costume to get some numbers, but I knew that Pikachu and Turbo games were the keys to reeling in the eligible bachelors around here."

Randy thanked the woman again and proceeded toward the door with Jay. As the two were about to exit the convention, Randy heard the cheerful music and 8-bit crowd sounds of an obscure NES game called *World Class Track Meet*. A group of people were huddled around an ancient, wood-paneled CRT that someone dug up from the back of the gym and were running in place on an NES PowerPad–a thin plastic mat with built-in pressure sensors that acted as a control mechanism for a small number of old Nintendo games. In this particular game, an on-screen runner would increase his sprint speed the harder and faster a player would run on the PowerPad. It was a simple, almost boring game in practice, but it was one of the earliest examples of motion gaming and it was surprisingly fun to play at parties or with friends and family. Randy had fond memories of his father digging out his old Nintendo from the closet on Christmas and hooking up the PowerPad to challenge him and his mother to races. His parents, drunk from holiday eggnog or wine, would prance around on the mat in loving competition and laugh in delight as their character celebrated a victory on the screen. They'd then let Randy run a race, cheering him on as he pumped his legs as fast as he could. Even though he had immersed himself in retro gaming for the better part of two decades, Randy hadn't thought about this game and these moments very often, as a palpable sadness would often arise when he reflected on his parents for any length of time. Today, however, he experienced a warm, comforting reminiscence and not a touch of melancholy as he watched the convention goers enjoying this oddity of a title. He was just happy that someone still owned the game, that a PowerPad was still working 40 years later, and that people could still derive pleasure from these early, experimental play mechanics of the 8-bit era.

"Fuck is that?" asked Jay.

"Nothing," said Randy. "Just memories."

9

Saturday had arrived. For the remainder of the week, after the intoxication of his romantic and emotional connection with Blake had begun to fade, Randy tried to convince himself to back out. At his most cynical points, he considered just not showing up at the protest, but he could not bring himself to back out without an explanation, and since he couldn't bring himself to call Blake and attempt an explanation, he knew that he had to go. He was sure that the protest would accomplish nothing, and knew that her desire to participate in it was fueled by an illusory idealism that would fade with age, especially if she stayed in the Corridor. He also knew that she was right when she referred to him as a guy without hope and when she implored him to search for something meaningful in his life. And thus he thought that going to the protest would, in some strange way, prove to Blake that her faith in him was not misplaced, and that he was capable of going beyond the horizon of his own interests and the intensity of his hesitations. In her presence, he felt more alive than he had in years and, while this feeling was connected to the fact that she was an attractive, twenty-year-old girl, it was something more than sexual desire that animated him. In their short time together, she demonstrated to him the power of uncompromised ideas and clarity of purpose. She was right about the utter contemptibility of faking the water contamination reports and about how people needed to act, and there was something liberating about being forced to confront a truth without having the time or opportunity to employ the gymnastics of intellectual abstraction that all too frequently disguise cowardice and apathy as cleverness. There was something exciting in her conviction that the power of creative self-expression could change lives, if only that of the creator. He hadn't engaged with ideas in this way since college and, even though the burden of life experience told him that this excitement was passing and its influence was limited, he could not ignore the seductive, visceral immediacy of joining Blake on this journey.

The text came from her just as the sun was setting. She asked him if he had found his Turbo Duo yet and he knew that he had an hour to get to Mercedes Drive. His biggest concern, ironically, was what to wear to the protest. His collection of video game t-shirts, sweaters and the mounds of old jeans in his room did not really fit the occasion, as they would be insulting to the cause and make him standout in the crowd, but he did not have many other options available to him. He finally chose a black, button-down shirt and a pair of brown slacks—an outfit that he used to wear, along with a brown tie, to job interviews, but which had been hanging in his closet, unneeded, for years. He combed his hair, brushed his teeth, and swallowed an antacid pill and two Xanax, before looking at himself in the mirror to double-check his appearance one last time. He thought it was silly that his anticipation at seeing Blake was stronger than his trepidation about what might happen to him and what he might suffer once the protest was broken up. If this group really did convince members of the foreign media to attend, then perhaps the protest would end with some simple demonstrations of force to disperse the crowd, along with a few fines. If not, then he expected most of the protesters to feel the sting of rubber bullets and the bite of multiple taser shots before they were arrested. An unfamiliar, chivalrous urge told him that, if he could just protect Blake from the worst reprisals of the security forces, be they steep fines or something more, he will have fulfilled his promise to her.

Randy had mapped out how he would arrive at the protest a few days earlier. At first he decided to park at an auto shop off of Carey Avenue and walk the five or so miles to the front gate of the housing development, but then he realized that whatever security forces would respond to the incident would probably travel that road, and he didn't want his car picked up by the drone sweeps of the area that would occur during and after the event. He decided instead to drive to one of the side streets close to the development, which itself was a kind of island surrounded by trees to the south, the river to the north and east, and security gates to the west. Based on what he could ascertain from an old paper map (he didn't have the courage to enter his destination into Google Maps), he could walk through the trees, across some old, unused railroad tracks, and then figure out a way in from there. Before leaving the house, he grabbed his backpack and, as the protesters instructed, placed a bottle of tap water in it, as well as some money, a utility knife, and a pair of gloves.

The streets were quiet and covered with patches of snow and ice that crackled under the weight of his tires. Even the intersection of Carey and Academy—one of the few places outside of downtown Wilkes-Barre that still had some residents and shops—was relatively free of traffic. Randy made a series of right turns and proceeded along the Susquehanna for a while, before snaking through a number of side streets lined with densely-packed rows of abandoned houses. He turned onto a road called Maffett Street and parked his car in the lot of what looked to be the remains of an old multi-family apartment house. It had no front door and the first floor windows had been shattered long ago, allowing ivy to grow up and into the building. There was a single light burning in the second floor window near the right end of the structure, which captured Randy's attention for a good minute and made him wonder if he should find another location to leave his car. Time was ticking, however, and he did not want Blake to think he was backing out, so he parked his car next to a rotted wooden fence, covered it with the tarp he kept in his tool box, and walked toward his destination.

The grove of trees which separated the housing development from the rest of the city proved to be thinner and easier to navigate than he had anticipated. There were, in fact, a few foot paths that had been made some time ago and were still usable. The difficulty came when he approached the railroad tracks in the middle of the grove and saw an imposing, eighteen-foot-tall steel fence just beyond them. It didn't have barbed wire or a fence topper to prevent climbing, but it was high, solid, and had smaller links than a standard chain link fence, which allowed less space for the fingers and toes of would-be climbers. Randy had not climbed a fence in years, and this fence would be a challenge even for someone experienced at the activity.

It took a few attempts to get his fingers in the right position to grip it before he could move upward in a slow, deliberate climb—trying to spread his legs and press the balls of his feet flat against the fence for increased stability and traction. The pressure on his fingers was immense, and his steady climb meant that his body was continually contorted in a position that caused his shoulder blades to ache. It became clear that the fence wasn't designed to prevent climbing, but simply to make it hurt enough that people would give up while they could still drop to the ground in relative safety.

Randy, however, did not have this option, so he soldiered on as his fingers began to bleed and his arms and neck started to go numb. He blocked out the pain and refused to look down until he could sling his arms over the top of the fence, which provided some relief, but allowed for the tips of the chain links to dig into the skin under his arms. He gripped the bar tightly and used his feet to push himself high enough to straddle the bar and hook it with his legs. This caused the full weight of his body to rest on his sternum and the lump of pressure in his chest to smolder into an explosive pain that forced him to let out a loud grunt, and with it a mixture of spit and blood that fell to the ground below. With an act of convulsive will, he slung his body to the other side and then resumed the painful grip with which he had scaled the front side of the fence, only this time it was harder to get his footing going downward and, because of this, he had to dig his hands further through the fence to support his body weight. He tried to focus his mental and physical energy on making a careful, deliberate descent, but he was quickly becoming exhausted and he felt his muscles getting rubbery. His fingers continually slipped through the links of the fence, forcing him to take frequent pauses to reposition himself and, once he became physically unable to continue the delicate path downward, he simply decided to drop to the ground in exhaustion.

He laid there for a while and gave himself over to a deep, wet cough. Out of pure instinct, he reached into his backpack and grabbed the bottle of faucet water that was intended for his target's lawn. Not knowing of any other way to contain the cough, he gulped it down, which helped him to catch his breath and suffer only the painful expansions and contractions of his ribcage.

Once recuperated enough to walk, he made his way through the remaining trees and came out near the intersection of Mercedes Drive and a small side street. The housing development was clean and every house seemed to be occupied, which was a rare sight in Wilkes-Barre. The houses were of a type popular in the mid-2000s—a kind of cookie-cutter, modern colonial style that impressed more with size than design. He made his way up the street and, as he traversed its mild incline, saw a group of people congregating and shouting in front of one of the larger houses, which was separated from the curb by a massive front yard and a large, horseshoe driveway.

The protesters numbered about fifty to sixty, and most of them had their water bottles and skull and cross bone shirts. They were huddled in front of the property chanting "Water is life!" and "The lies end tonight!" Randy began to wade through the crowd to look for Blake, but he couldn't spot her. As he continued his search, moving from the perimeter of the crowd to its center, he was stopped by a large man wearing a ski mask.

"You with us?" he barked.

"Yeah," replied Randy, "I'm just looking for my friend."

"Nice, dude," he said, extending his hand. "We on the right side of history tonight, man. This motherfucker knew he was fuckin' poisoning everyone left in the city and he didn't give a fuck!"

"I heard," said Randy, "That's totally fucked up."

"Damn straight. Did you read that report?"

Randy hesitated, as he did not read every word of the SkinFlick message when Blake showed it to him.

"Kind of," he said.

"Man, this rat bastard got, like, bonuses and shit. The higher he got them contamination levels, the more he made. I mean, he got like a mil last year.

And meanwhile my baby was born with fuckin' brain damage. Man, fuck him."

Another man came up to them. He was wearing a heavy scarf and a gray pea-coat and seemed to be monitoring something on his phone.

"That's why we have to fight, gentlemen," he said, "We are taking this battle to every major city in the Corridor and beyond and we're going to let people know that 15% of America's population is being cruelly and deliberately poisoned in the name of profit. Give me your phone numbers if you're not in the database already."

"I'm in, man" said the man in the mask.

Randy hesitated, but then gave the organizer his phone number, which he wrote down on a note pad.

"Spread the word," he told Randy. "The days of suffering in silence end tonight."

Randy again stepped back and tried to find Blake but, even though the crowd had grown, he could not see her. He staked out a position on the opposite side of the street, which was a bit more elevated and provided a better view of the protest, but it was to no avail. He noticed that people in the neighboring houses were standing in the windows and that the huddled protesters, now chanting louder, started moving onto the lawn of the property. Dejected, Randy joined the back end of the group that remained on the side walk and checked his phone, but there were no messages.

After standing in silence for a while, a heavy-set woman approached him and poked him in the chest, making him wince.

"Where's your bottle?" she bellowed.

"I forgot mine," said Randy.

"Fuck, man. Hold this." She shoved a glass bottle filled with water into his hands while she reached into her handbag and took out a white towel.

"Gimme that," she said, grabbing the bottle back and stuffing the towel in it, which she wet with water from another bottle.

"Fuck are you doing?" asked Randy.

The woman cackled. "The other day my son showed me how to set our tap water on fire, so I'm gonna light this and see what fuckin' happens."

"I don't think that's the point of the protest," said Randy.

"Be a little chicken shit if you want! I'll get this fucker's attention for the both of us," she said, wedging herself into the center of the crowd.

The organizer now had a mega phone and began to direct the group into orderly rows. He then turned to the house and began speaking.

"For years, Geo Services Corporation has been paying the City of Wilkes-Barre to knowingly falsify its water contamination reports. Every resident of the city who has ever drank this water has greatly increased his or her chances of developing a host of chronic illnesses that can cause premature death. Children who drink this water suffer from irreversible brain damage. This must end. What is water?"

The crowd shouted, "Water is life!"

"So tonight, we stand in solidarity and protest," he continued. "I ask all who have joined me tonight to take out their tap water and pour it onto this man's lawn. Let it serve as an example of our rejection of corruption and our refusal to allow ourselves and our families to be poisoned. What is water?

"Water is life!" the crowd again responded

As people began to pour their water onto the flowerbeds that surrounded the mailbox, Randy could hear the faint wail of sirens and saw four patrol drones approaching from the other end of the street. The chants continued and the protesters became more irritable, with several veering off the script and shouting epithets at the target's family, the city council, and the U.S. government. The woman with the makeshift Molotov cocktail moved to the front of the group and lit the rag, which caught fire more quickly than she expected.

She shouted "My water is death!" as she tossed the fiery projectile on the lawn and watched it burst into flames. Another man ran to the flowerbed and slammed down a lit book of matches, which created a carpet of fire that consumed the flowers and the mailbox. Several other protesters with bandannas over their mouths ran towards the house with their own Molotov cocktails and threw them through the windows, as other protesters screamed "Burn baby burn!" and did not respond to the organizer's requests for civility.

The police sirens drew nearer, and the group devolved into a general state of panic as the flames began to climb up the house and cover more of the lawn. A few people tried to run back to the entry gate, but then doubled back to the house and claimed that there was a riot squad moving towards their location. Another handful tried to escape down the opposite end of the street, but were stopped from escaping by a large drone which blocked their path and scanned them with a pale, red light. They also rushed back to the house, which by now was beyond saving. Randy backed away from the group, as he sensed that they were being contained there and would be the first target of police aggression. A second, larger drone approached from the direction of the entry gate and began scanning the crowd with its own light. The organizer tried to calm the protesters and guide them in what to say when they were arrested but, with a quick puff of air and a flash of light from the drone above, he was shot in the head, causing him to drop to his knees, double over, and bleed out onto the street.

The protesters began screaming and scattering in every direction. Randy followed a few men who were sprinting toward the grove of trees, but one of the drones swooped down in front of them and picked off two of the men in the group, before ascending again and heading back to the house. Randy could see flashing police lights in front of him and instinctively ran away, back towards the protest, where he saw the riot police tasing people and beating them with batons. Another group of armed officers were placing black bags over the heads of certain people who had already been beaten to the ground. They bound their hands and feet with zip ties and dragged them off to a van that was parked on a side street. They worked with a quick, selective efficiency that stood in stark contrast to the frantic bludgeoning of the normal police force.

The question in Randy's mind was not whether he would be caught, but what fate he would suffer. He banded together with some of the last remaining people who had managed to escape harm and walked, with hands raised, in a slow march back towards the gate. As they moved towards the police barricade, stepping over the bodies of the protesters who had been killed by the drones, they came upon a woman who was on her knees, crying in the street. Five officers approached her with guns drawn.

"Drop your weapon!" they shouted.

"I don't have a weapon!" she shouted back.

An officer stepped forward from the group to address her.

"Ma'am, I will not ask you again. Please put down the weapon!"

"I don't have a weapon!" she screamed, her voice cracking into loud, sickening sobs.

The officer reached for the microphone on his shoulder and calmly said, "Note for the record that the suspect will not surrender her weapon."

The woman took off her coat and laid it down in front of her. She raised her hands to the sky and screamed again. "I don't have a weapon! Please God I don't have anything!"

The officer walked closer to her, with his hand gun at his side. She looked up at him, crying uncontrollably.

"I don't have a weapon," she said.

The officer knelt down in front of her and rubbed her shoulder.

"I asked you to put down your weapon," he said in a softer tone. Then he shot her three times in the stomach.

As she slumped down into a fetal position on the pavement, he grabbed his microphone again and stated, "Please note that the threat has been eliminated." He stood up and shot her once more in the head before approaching Randy and the remaining members of his group.

"You gentlemen are under arrest," he said, signaling to the other officers to move in.

"On the ground! Face down! Hands on the back of your head!" shouted another officer. Everyone complied.

Before he knew it, Randy was in the back of a police car heading to the Luzerne County Jail in central Wilkes-Barre. It was unclear why he and the people he was with were treated well compared to the woman killed in the street or the men killed by the drones. He thought perhaps it was because he had not been standing near the Molotov cocktail throwers or that he had the good fortune of running in the right directions, at the right times. Or perhaps, he surmised, mass brutality resisted rational categories, and that, by some twist of fate, he was left alive to face the consequences of the protest while others were killed in the street. The truly torturous thought, however, was that Blake could have been a victim of the violence. He was sure that she wasn't there at the start of the night, but as the chaos ensued, he couldn't be absolutely certain that she hadn't arrived at some later point; and, as he was sure that his possessions would be seized at the jail, he would not be able to call and check on her for the foreseeable future. He was overcome by the aching realization that he had vowed to protect her and yet he wasn't even able to locate her. Instead of searching the crowd multiple times, of calling her nonstop, of finding the courage to call Jay and ask where she was, he instead stood on the sidelines and watched as the world around him went to hell. If they both somehow managed to survive this ordeal and see each other again on the outside, he knew that his crippling failure could never be forgiven.

10

Randy found it curious that his arrest didn't follow the ubiquitous patterns established by crime shows and movies. He wasn't read his Miranda rights before being dragged off, his possessions weren't seized when he was processed at the jail, there was no finger printing, no offer of a phone call, and no interrogation. He was simply led to a crowded holding cell and left there without instructions or any indication of what would happen next.

The cell was larger than one would imagine a prison cell to be, but it was packed full with about 30 people, some of whom were protesters, but also many others who seemed to have been there for much longer. There were two beds on opposite sides of the cell and a metal toilet on the back wall. Randy felt a strong urge to vomit, and he could feel a bloody cough building within him, but the cell was so jam packed that he couldn't turn around, let alone get to the toilet. He was one of the last ones to be locked inside and his body was pressed against the steel bars of the door, which added to the pain in his chest. He was trapped in the kind of bureaucratically induced claustrophobia that forced people into an unnatural proximity with each other and held them there without mercy, until the machinations of some opaque process were complete, only in this instance the process itself was unknown and, in the absence of any information, the ordeal became maddening.

Randy looked down and saw a man with blood red eyes leaning against his right leg, mumbling incoherently.

He nudged him and asked, "You know how long we've got to be here?

The man looked up at him as if he didn't understand the question, then, furrowing his brow in an apparent act of contemplation, said, "Not sure. I prolly been here for days, man."

Randy felt deflated, but hoped the man was mistaken.

"Days?" asked Randy. "What about meals? Showers? Aren't they supposed to bring you into the general population or something?"

The man seemed confused again.

"I dunno about that," he said, as if trying to recall an experience that would confirm or deny Randy's presumptions. "I mean, they bring us food. Like a candy bar or summin."

A man called out to Randy from behind.

"At least you up front, motherfucker! I can't breathe back here, man! You wanna fuckin' switch?"

Time passed, but Randy wasn't sure how long he had been in the cell. It was long enough for him to become inured to the stench of desperate humanity and for the reverberations of the silent scream of near insanity to fade from his mind. He had made a transition from living to simply existing, draping his arms over the bars and staring at the cubicle in the middle of the holding area, but not really taking notice of who was working in it or what they were doing. This transition might have happened in hours or it could have been days, but the exact time mattered less and less in this state of persistent suffering.

Eventually prisoners were released. Some were processed again and taken into the main prison itself. Others were bailed out by a spouse or child. Randy, however, was removed from his cell and placed with several other prisoners, a few of them protestors, in an office off of the holding area. They were neither cuffed nor supervised. Randy wanted to speak to a man he recognized from the protest, but he looked ill and lost in his own world, and Randy himself felt that futile attempts at speech were a waste of his waning energy. He looked at his phone, which was just about dead but did have reception in this room, and saw a flood of unimportant emails rush in. Nothing from Blake. It was 2:00pm on Monday.

After an hour of sitting in silence, an officer entered the room and said, "Alright, your cases have been reviewed and you're being transferred to the Oakvale Rehabilitation Center. I am handing you your release papers. Sign them. Hold on to them. Transportation to the facility costs $39.95. Have your debit cards out. If you do not have funds for the transfer, you'll be returned to our facility. Any questions?"

Everyone remained silent. The officer went around the room handing out release paperwork and swiping debit cards. Once he was done, he ushered the group through a dark corridor and out to the rear of the prison, where an old yellow school bus was waiting. They boarded and the driver was given the ok to depart. The bus drove onto Bridge Street, but then turned back and made its way through several residential streets near the prison complex and back onto Courtright Avenue, where the rehabilitation facility was ultimately located. As they got off the bus, they could still see one of the prison towers from the parking lot.

WHEN THEY ENTERED the Oakvale Rehabilitation Center, they were taken into what looked to be a dining hall, but the tables were gone and replaced with cots. On each cot was a small pillow and a plastic bag that read "Welcome" and had the names of the new arrivals written on a sticker. Randy searched for his bag and discovered a tooth brush, soap, a bath towel, a disposable razor, a pair of generic athletic shorts and a t-shirt inside of it.

A woman in a white coat entered to address the group.

"Welcome to Oakvale!" she said, "I know you've all gone through some pretty tough ordeals over the past week, so I'd like you all to shower up, enjoy a hot meal and, most importantly, get some sleep!"

The new arrivals lined up in alphabetical order for their showers. The shower stalls were private and seemed to be new. Randy couldn't remember the last time he'd gone for so long without cleaning himself and, as he allowed the pleasant, warm water to cascade over him, he imagined the stench of the prison and the trauma of the protest falling away from his mind. He showered for ten minutes, shaved, and brushed his teeth.

The mirror above the sink in the bathroom was large and in it he was able to notice the continual deterioration of his body, which was revealed in great detail on account of the bright florescent lighting of the room. His eyes were sunken in and his face was paler than he'd ever seen it. He noticed that his hairline had receded even more over the past two weeks, such that the majority of the hair he had left was concentrated in his ponytail. He had lost some noticeable definition in the muscles of his upper body and the skin on his chest and stomach had a yellowish tint. His legs had become boney, with his once full quadriceps muscles shriveling and inching closer to his hips.

He left the bathroom dressed in the t-shirt and shorts he had received in his gift bag and returned to the dining room, where he found a tray of food on his cot. It was a mixture of shredded chicken with a bland, viscous white gravy and a side of mashed potatoes and green beans. It would have seemed unappealing in former times, but Randy was so crippled with hunger that he devoured it as fast as his hands and mouth could coordinate with each other. His now common struggle to keep food down didn't matter to him, as he happily mixed new bites of food with whatever material found its way back into his mouth and swallowed it all again with desperate pleasure. Full, clean, and exhausted, he laid down on his cot and, feeling human for the first time since his arrest, was able to sleep.

THE NEXT DAY BEGAN with the woman in the white coat coming into the dining room and flicking the lights on and off to rouse the new arrivals. Breakfast was wheeled in by three or four orderlies, and the arrivals were asked to leave their dirty clothes in a mound for the laundry service. Everyone was given an hour to eat and wash up, and then told to proceed down the hall and wait in the foyer for processing. Randy found it strange that he would be going to a meeting in little more than his pajama-like shorts and t-shirt combo, but he complied.

The foyer was a large, bright room with comfortable furniture and lots of plants and small trees arranged in symmetrical patterns. There were fish tanks near the reception area and a caged parrot, which sat near the entrance to the room and looked out quizzically at the guests. After about an hour of waiting, the receptionist called Randy's name and escorted him into an office, where a man, perhaps a bit younger than he was, sat behind a glossy executive desk.

"Mr. James," he said, standing up and extending his hand. "My name is Carlos and I'll be your RSR." He paused for a moment to see if Randy understood the acronym's meaning, then said, "Rehabilitation

Services Rep. Please have a seat. By the way, if you want to charge your phone, just plug it in over there at the end of the desk."

Randy sat down and plugged his phone into the USB charging cable which poked out from the edge of the desk.

"I know you probably have a lot of questions about why you were sent here and what you'll be doing here, so I'm going to briefly go over our mission here at Oakvale and then take down some more specific information. After that, I'll be happy to answer any questions you may have. Sound good?"

Randy nodded.

"Ok. Great. Basically what we do here is handle crime prevention for the city. The police will typically pick someone up or identify someone on a patrol and conduct an analysis of the available data surrounding that person. In your case, this happened after the incident on Saturday night. When that analysis identifies someone as leaning in a potentially criminal direction, they're usually brought here to our rehabilitation program. Our goal is to help people correct certain behaviors and teach them to make positive choices so that they can avoid actual incarceration."

"And this is just because of what I did on Saturday?" asked Randy.

"Well, Saturday was a major data point, yes. The police report also indicates that you work as a hauler, but put in nowhere near the max hours, so that was the second data point. According to the police, this combination of free time and your decision to attend an event that ended in criminal violence made you a strong candidate for rehabilitation."

"So I fuck up once and I get locked up?" asked Randy.

"Well, that was my next point," Carlos continued. "This is not jail. You were not accused or convicted of any crime. You were simply exercising your First Amendment rights and you did not engage in any of the violence that ensued, so you've done nothing wrong. I want to make that clear. We're here to help you. You can move about the complex freely. You'll have lots of opportunity for work and recreational activities. You can call friends and family and have them visit you. This is by no means a punishment. Just a chance to re-evaluate your choices and put yourself in a more positive place so that you can avoid dangerous situations in the future."

"And how long do I have to stay here?" asked Randy.

"Well, we make that determination after seeing how well you complete the program. Sometimes it can last for a week or two, sometimes longer."

"And what exactly is the program?"

"I'll get to that. First, though, I want to ask you some questions about Saturday. Ok?"

"Fine."

"So let's come back to the protest. That was a pretty serious situation. I mean, you gotta be really connected to even find out about something like that. How did you hear about it?"

Randy tried hard to repress a smirk, as he was not going to compromise himself or Blake so easily.

"Some guys were talking about it at work," he said.

"Any names?" asked Carlos, raising an eyebrow.

"Nah, just some guys at work. At a rest stop."

"But that's not the sort of thing haulers usually talk about, right?" asked Carlos. "I mean, it seems like an odd topic for a bunch of guys making their living in the energy industry."

"Haulers talk about a lot of things," said Randy.

"See that's the thing though," said Carlos, now with clear suspicion in his voice, "according to reports we have, the group that organized this protest was the Green Front. They're a borderline terrorist organization and they don't really post their activities everywhere. You gotta know someone on the inside to find out about something like this. My guess is that haulers don't typically have contact with environmental terrorist groups."

"Well, maybe the guys I heard it from were on the inside," said Randy, "I don't know though. I just listened to them and didn't ask questions. I've never heard of the Green Front or anything like that."

"Ok. Ok. But what I wanna know is, how do you make the jump?" asked Carlos.

"The jump?"

"Yeah, how do you make the jump from hearing something to actually going out to this thing? I mean, reports indicate that you live alone, you keep to yourself, you don't have a history of civil disobedience or criminal behavior. How do you just decide one night to go to this protest and put yourself at risk?"

Randy shrugged his shoulders.

"I'm getting older," Randy said, "I guess I just wanted to make one last stupid decision."

Carlos chuckled in an attempt to mask his mild irritation.

"Alright, man. One last question" he said. "Says here you get this life insurance payment every month, plus you're on the city profit sharing plan, which nets you another thousand. That's a nice chunk of change. But if you worked max hours at hauling, you could be clearing like eighty grand a year in total. Most people around here would kill for that kind a money. Why haven't you taken advantage of the chance to bank that?"

Randy was not expecting this question and could not think of a reasonable answer, knowing only that he did not want to reveal anything about his hobbies or the game room.

"Laziness," he said, "That and I guess I always thought I'd find another gig outside of hauling."

"Ok. I hear you, man" said Carlos, making a note on the manila folder in front of him. "Now, let's talk about the program. We basically just want to put you in what we call an evaluation program. It's gonna focus on social skills and some job skills. Pretty basic, really."

"And how long does it go for?" asked Randy.

"Again, the length of your stay depends totally on your progress."

"No, I mean, how long is the evaluation period? How long will you be testing me before you get an idea of where I'm at?" asked Randy with noticeable frustration.

"Well, I wouldn't look at it as testing you," said Carlos, "We just want you to live normally. Take advantage of what we offer here. Engage with people. You'll be fine."

Randy sighed.

"So here is what you'll do," said Carlos. "We're going to assign you a roommate. Just see if you can live with him. Make a connection. Communicate and develop strategies for sharing the space. And we're going to put you in our basic job skills course."

"And what does that entail?"

"Well, three days a week you are going to head over to our call center and work some basic tech support. You'll field calls from cable customers on the West Coast and help them with basic stuff like setting up their accounts, email, helping them with lost passwords, things like that. You'll work about ten hours a day on average, sometimes a little less if the call volume is low."

"I have to work for you guys!" asked Randy, his voice hovering somewhere between a grunt and a scream.

"Well, you're not working for us. We've partnered with Gold Coast Cable Systems to give our residents a chance to learn some job skills. This is how we test your interpersonal communication skills and assess how well you handle multi-step instruction sets. Plus, you'll earn about $8.00 an hour after fees, so you'll have some pocket money to buy stuff here. Most of our residents like the opportunity."

"So, basically, I don't have any choice in any of this?"

"Now, I wouldn't see it that way, man," said Carlos, with a note of exacerbation in his voice. "This is a chance to heal. A chance to make a course correction in your life and learn how to interact positively with people. You just need to keep an open mind. Stop complaining about what's happening *to* you and focus on what can happen *for* you."

Randy knew that continuing the exchange was pointless, so he cleared his throat and stared back at Carlos.

"Anyway," Carlos continued, "The last step is to talk about payment. Now, most of your stay is covered by your Extended Medicaid Plan, but you're gonna be responsible for the remainder of the fee."

"How much is that?" asked Randy. "I don't have a ton of savings."

"Well, we don't dip into our residents' savings. We are just going to ask that you divert your annuity and profit sharing payments to us for the duration of your stay. It's completely automatic and includes all recreational activities, medical treatments, and Internet access."

Randy's initial anger settled into a feeling of helplessness as Carlos handed him a packet of paperwork to sign. It was clear that there was no alternative other than to accept the terms offered to him and hope that he could get out in a few weeks.

"Just initial up top and sign and date the bottom of each page, and we're good to go," said Carlos.

Randy complied.

"Thanks, Randy," said Carlos, "I'm happy you're staying with us and I think we can really help you. Here's your Internet access code and your ID. You're gonna be staying in room 157. Just turn left outside my office and follow the hallway 'til you see it. I'll follow up in a few days to see how you're doing."

They shook hands. Randy grabbed his cell phone and left to find his room. As he walked through the hall, he felt nauseated by the building's repressive sterility. It appeared to have been a former nursing home or a hospital annex, with wide, polished floors, unmanned nurse's stations, and gurneys lining the hallway. Huge florescent tube lights ran the entire length of the ceiling, casting everything in a greenish glow, and there was a pervasive scent of industrial strength cleaners that struggled to mask undertones of urine and feces.

Randy felt consumed by an almost vertiginous disgust when he arrived at his room, the door to which was open and had his name written in purple marker below the number placard. Upon entering, he saw two small hospital beds, a wall-mounted TV across from them, and a large window with open blinds on the far side of the room. To his left was a large, hospital-style bathroom with a shower and a toilet upon which, to Randy's surprise, sat a large Hispanic man. His gut was poking out from beneath his t-shirt, his arms looked like bulging, muscular tree trunks and his pants were around his ankles.

"Hey, man," he said, extending his hand to Randy for a shake, "Name's Antonio."

Randy obliged with a quick handshake.

"Guess we're roomies," said Antonio.

"Yeah," said Randy, moving into the room and identifying his bed, which was closest to the window and had his belongings hanging in a plastic bag from the bedpost.

Randy sat down and checked his phone. Still nothing from Blake. The only messages he had received were a few notifications from his bank authorizing the transfer of funds from his account to Oakvale's.

THROUGHOUT THE NEXT TEN DAYS, Randy established an unflinching routine. He'd wake up at six, shower, shave, and then walk down to a small cafeteria area to have breakfast. The menu was always the same: two whole wheat waffles, an egg, and a strip of bacon. Water was complimentary, but residents could purchase coffee or orange juice from a vending machine.

On Mondays, Wednesdays, and Fridays he would head down to a conference area in the basement and work his call center job. The room had four rows of plastic folding tables, each with a laptop and a head set for taking calls. He would sit there and answer basic account information requests and tech support questions from customers in San Francisco and Los Angeles. He found it amusing that, despite a solid 25 years since the advent of Internet 2.0, people still couldn't figure out how to sign up for email or check their monthly bandwidth reports. Because of his basic technical proclivity, he found the job rather easy and was often rewarded with an extra dollar here or there when the computer system recognized that he was exceeding the average hourly call volume by a certain percentage. This kind of performance stood in stark contrast to his other co-workers, some of whom were older and unsure of how to use the computer system properly. Others could not speak English fluently enough to be understood, and there were some workers who seemed to suffer from severe psychological and cognitive deficits that made them completely ineffective at their jobs and resulted in staff members entering the room and taking copious notes to document their struggles. When the work day was over, he would stick his ID card into a machine at the entrance to the room, which showed him statistics on his work performance and deposited his modest pay into his Oakvale account.

On days when he didn't have to work, he would go to the library and read or do some light cardio work in the gym. Dinners were the responsibility of the residents, and they had the choice of joining a cooking group and preparing a large meal for all of the members, or they could go to a commissary on the second floor, which had a variety of fast-food dishes to choose from, almost all of which were sold at airport prices. Randy would choose the second option and spend an hour or two picking at a hamburger and checking his phone. It still pained him that he had heard nothing from Blake, and even when he tried to call her, all he got was her voicemail. Slowly, however, the calming predictability of his routine, coupled with his complete powerlessness to change it, made the sadness of the protest seem distant and his life of relaxed detainment almost tolerable.

Once the commissary closed down, Randy would return to his room, where Antonio was usually sitting on his bed, watching college football. Twice a week, Oakvale staff would come by with portable VR headsets and offer residents "calming personal experiences" for $1 per minute. The content included a beach scene, a tour of a famous landmark, or a trip through space. There were also some simple games and puzzles that could be played and even some softcore pornography that offered patients a chance to relieve some of their sexual tension. Randy used the headsets occasionally and gravitated to 3D Tetris, which was always available and fun as ever. Antonio, however, paid for VR every time it was offered and would lay on his bed masturbating for the better part of an hour.

At first, Randy didn't bother talking to Antonio, as he was loud, crude, and dominated the room without a second thought. Randy knew, beyond any stretch of the imagination, that Antonio was the alpha male of the pair and that conflict did not make sense. As time wore on, however, he would engage him in small talk or ask about the details of the football games he was watching. He wasn't sure how Carlos or other members of the Oakvale staff could prove that he was trying to communicate with his roommate, but he figured it was worth a try if it increased his chances of leaving the facility.

One night, when the topics of basic chit-chat had been exhausted and the silence between them grew awkward, Randy decided to initiate a more serious conversation.

"What are you in here for?" he asked, thinking it a fair question for those being kept at a facility dedicated to crime prevention.

Antonio seemed surprised that Randy had chosen the topic, but was happy to chat.

"I'm in here cause I got angry at a bank," he said.

"What?" said Randy. "How could they possibly put you in here for that?"

"Well, it went down like this. I was in there trying to get my money from an ATM, and it said my account was overdrawn or some shit. So I talked to the manager. And I was like, 'My account ain't overdrawn.' He was like, 'Sir, it is.' And I was like, 'Dude, it isn't.' And then he asked me to leave. So, I told him I'd come back with a machete and cut him up and eat his heart in front of his kids."

"Fuck," said Randy, unsure of how to react to what he had just heard. "And he called the cops on you?"

"Nah, man," said Antonio, "they got me sayin' it on the security feed or something and they grabbed me at home that night and brought me here."

"They just busted into your house?"

"Basically. It was probably for the best though, cause I was googling machetes when they came in. How'd you wind up here, dude?"

"Well," said Randy, relieved that the conversation was moving in another direction, "I was at this protest and things went to shit and I got arrested."

"Protest?" asked Antonio. "That's fucking stupid, man. I mean, going to a protest is like walking down the street with a sign that says 'Hey, over here! Cluster-fuck my life!'"

"Yeah, well, it was dumb, but I didn't think it would be as bad as it was. I mean, I assumed the police would come and I'd get fined or some shit, but I didn't think it would be as bloody as it was and I didn't think I'd end up here."

"Bloody?" said Antonio, with uncomfortable intrigue. "What happened?"

"Well, a couple of people threw these Molotov cocktail things at this guy's house. Went up in flames. The police were called. They sent in these drones that were fucking shooting people from the sky. Riot police were tazing and beating people. Cops shot some others. Then these other guys were, like, putting bags over peoples' heads and dragging them away. Pretty fucked up."

"Fuck, man, they called the Erasers? That's some serious shit."

"Erasers?" asked Randy.

"Yeah man, you never heard of the Erasers?"

"No, what're they?"

"They're like private security that work for the police. They basically haul your ass off if they don't want to arrest you. Happened to my brother."

"What the fuck? How is that even possible?" asked Randy.

"Well, look at it this way," said Antonio. "You were at the protest. They arrested you. You spent some time in the can and then they released you here. I popped off at some motherfucker in a bank. I'm here. Where are the motherfuckers who got bagged?"

"Who's to say they aren't in prison?" asked Randy.

"My brother ain't in prison."

"What happened to him?"

"Well, my brother was like a broke junkie and shit. Like real bad. He did time for robbery, but when he got out, he went right back to the street, stealing copper from old central air units around town and sellin' it to get high. One night, I went with him to a strip club outside of Scranton and we left real late and we got jumped in the parking lot. The guys tased me and they tied up my brother– hands and feet–and then they put this bag over his head and threw him in to the back of a van. Boom. Gone. I went to the jail the next day to see if I could bail him out and they were like 'Who? No records, sir.' Real fucked up shit."

"Fuck," said Randy. "How the fuck is that even legal? I mean, I know the police are bastards, but people still have rights."

"It probably ain't legal," said Antonio, "But a guy like my brother has nothing, so there ain't no

145

consequence to it. His girl was a crack whore. I ain't got no money for a lawyer. Who's gonna complain?"

"But what I don't get is, why did they take him and yet you and I are here?" asked Randy, still not convinced by the explanation. "How the fuck do they decide who gets erased and who gets to be rehabilitated?"

"Money, man" answered Antonio, "plain and fuckin' simple. They called my moms and asked her if she was willing to hand over her social security to keep me here. They called my wife and told her they would take half her monthly salary to keep me here. Both of them said yes. My moms moved in with my wife, so here I am. That and I ain't never actually been caught for no crime. Way I see it, you gotta have that combo. No convictions and some money, then you come here."

"That's just fucking unbelievable," said Randy. "I mean, I can't believe no one tries to stop this. There's gotta be another explanation. I mean, what the fuck kind of a place are we living in?"

"Easy one, man," said Antonio. "Fuckin' Wilkes-Barre. If I'd a had any fuckin skills at all, I'd a left this shit hole. But I didn't. No college. No nothing. So what do I got left? I was working demolition. My girl works in an office. We were getting by. Then I fucked up, but my girls are keepin' me alive in here. If I get out, I'll try to repay'em. If not, well, the money runs out and I run out. This city's the final destination, man. We're all checkin' out. Just a matter of when."

11

Randy collapsed at breakfast. He was struggling to get down small bites of the dry, whole wheat waffles that were the Oakvale morning staple, when he felt his throat close up. At first, he sensed the normal gurgling from within his chest that had become a typical accompaniment to his meals, but as he slowly and methodically attempted to finish what was on his plate, the gurgling stopped and it seemed as if the food and liquid were gathering in an ever expanding bubble that pushed up into his throat. He started coughing, then tried to vomit, but couldn't relieve the pressure. He began heaving and gasping for air as a cold sweat built within his pores. His chin developed an involuntary quiver and, feeling dizzy and weak, he dropped to the floor on his hands and knees, pulling his stomach inward with all of his might in an attempt to loosen whatever was depriving him of air. Time seemed to stop and he could see small drops of blood landing on the worn tiles of the cafeteria floor with each retch of his stomach.

He woke up on the gantry of a CT scanner. He was groggy and attempted to sit up to orient himself to his new surroundings. A nurse rushed in from behind him, gently pressed his head back onto the pillow, and held his right hand while making a gentle shushing sound. Another nurse started an IV in his left arm and hooked it up to a portable white machine with two cylinders containing a clear liquid.

"You'll be fine," said one of the nurses. "We're just going to take some pictures of your stomach."

They left the room and the machine began to whir. The gantry moved his body forward and backward, pausing at certain intervals and telling him to "Breathe in and hold" in a computerized voice. After the process ended, the machine said "Injection" and he could feel the tubes of his IV stiffen as something was injected into his arm, causing his cheeks to go flush and a warm, stinging sensation to build in his groin. He was then moved back and forth through the machine a second time.

"What happened to me?" asked Randy, as the nurses were unhooking his IV.

A nurse stared down at him with a look of compassion and pity.

"We'll send these films to the doctor and he'll discuss them with you a bit later," she said, rubbing his arm.

Before leaving the exam room, he was given two pills and told only to drink liquids until he met with the doctor. Randy walked back to his room, using the wooden railings that lined the hallways to balance himself, as he still felt nauseous and dizzy. Antonio saw him struggling to maintain his balance and helped him get into the room and make his way to the bed, offering a fist bump before he left for his work shift. Randy grabbed the cup of water next to his bed and swallowed the two pills which, within minutes, produced an almost euphoric sense of relaxation. He slept soundly through the afternoon and night.

RANDY AWOKE THE NEXT DAY feeling refreshed and energized. As was his routine, he walked down to the cafeteria and found a protein shake on his table instead of the usual breakfast, which he drank down in a swift gulp, before ordering two strong coffees from the vending machine. Because of his choking episode, he was removed from work duty until further notice and thus decided to head down to the commissary and spend his day on the Internet. As he was passing the foyer, he was shocked to see Blake sitting on one of the couches, dressed in baggy pajamas, her knees tucked into her chest as she was reading on her phone.

He walked over to her.

"Blake?" he asked in disbelief.

She looked up at him with delayed surprise and a hint of sadness.

"Oh my god," she said, eventually throwing her arms around his neck and holding the embrace for longer than was normal, as if to verify to her senses that he really was standing in front of her.

"What are you doing here?" asked Randy.

She looked around to see if anyone was close enough to hear her.

"They got me at the protest and put me in here," she said in a half whisper.

"You were there?"

Blake looked around again and noticed the receptionist lift her head and glance in their direction.

"It's a long story. Let's go somewhere else," she said.

They walked passed the receptionist, who smiled at them as they proceeded toward the main corridor of the first floor. Randy suggested going to the commissary, but Blake insisted on going to the third floor, on which her room was located and which she thought was more private. As they stood in the elevator, she took his hand in hers and held it tightly, while the subtle jostling of the ride upward shifted their bodies closer together.

The third floor was, as Blake had predicted, virtually empty, and they walked unnoticed into a recreation room at the far end of one of the hallways. They both grabbed a coffee from the vending machine in the room and sat down, facing each other on a small sofa. The blinds in the room were open and the sunlight revealed the beauty of her supple, milky white skin. Her lips were chapped as ever and her eyes, though encircled with regions of dark puffiness, still had the playful effervescence that Randy found irresistible. He only hoped that the daylight would be kind to his fading appearance which, he believed, must have further deteriorated after his choking episode yesterday.

Blake sipped her coffee and stroked Randy's face with the tips of her knuckles.

"I can't believe we found each other here," she said.

"So what happened that night?" asked Randy. "I was so worried about you."

She inhaled deeply, her breath tense as it was drawn in.

"It's so fucking embarrassing, actually," she said. "I was late. I was actually late. This was so fucking important to me and I couldn't get there on time. I was about to leave, and Jay wouldn't let me go and we had this fight and I just…I just got there late."

"So, I mean, did you see anything?" asked Randy.

"Not really. I got to the gate and there was this line-up of police and I knew I wasn't going to get through, and when they saw me they told me to stop, but I just started running and they shot me with this stun gun or something," she said, twisting her back towards Randy and pulling up her shirt to reveal two grayish-brown circular scars above her right hip.

"Fucking cops," Randy said. "They could have just let you run with all the other shit going on."

"I knew going in that I was probably going to get arrested or something, but I really wanted to be there and contribute before it happened. I feel like I let myself down and everyone else. Fucking pathetic, when you think about it."

"Come on," said Randy, "There was nothing you could have done once the cops got there."

"Yeah, well, the worst part of it is the cops took my phone when they arrested me. I just hope they don't figure out what group I was connected to and catch everyone because of my fuck up."

Randy considered asking her about the group and why she had agreed to join them, but decided against it, as he wasn't sure if there was a camera in the room and didn't want to put her in any further danger.

"It was better that you weren't there anyway," Randy said. "It got out of control so fast. Total shit show."

"What happened?"

He was tempted to vent about the fire, the beatings and the killings, but decided to spare her the gory details, partly because he himself didn't want to suffer the pain of recollection.

"Well, we sent a strong message," said Randy. "There was an accident though at the guy's house and it wound up catching fire. Then the cops came and things went to hell. Lots of arrests and lots of violence."

"Were the guys from Cincinnati there?" she asked.

Randy didn't know who the Cincinnati participants were for sure, but he assumed the organizer who was executed by the drone was one of them. This small margin of uncertainty, however, allowed him to give a safe answer.

"I'm not sure. It was pretty chaotic and I didn't really talk to anyone."

"Did anyone get killed?" she asked.

"Yeah. Some protesters did."

Blake stared at the floor in disgust.

"I really hate this place," she whispered. "This whole fucking world is a disease, and it's like it consumes you bit by bit."

"That's not true," Randy said. "It's fucked up here, yeah, but you can still get out and live your life somewhere else."

"Stop with that rosy-eyed bullshit," she replied, in an aggressive, angry tone of which Randy did not think her capable. "It sucks everywhere. This fucking Corridor is the worst, but the rest of this fucking world isn't that much better."

Randy could not formulate a rebuttal that wouldn't sound patronizing or pedantic, so he attempted to brush the hair away from her eyes. She pulled back and slapped his hand away.

"All I wanted to do was be part of something," she said, almost screaming, "Be part of a movement that tells this system to go fuck itself. I wanted to do it just once, and now my chance is gone! People died for this and I was late, like a fucking child."

Randy felt himself pushed to the limits of his ability to read her. Her words contained a blunt insight and accuracy that he could neither ignore nor dispute, and he knew that his attempts to assuage her fears and allay her criticisms with common sense and positive thinking were conceptually bankrupt. Yet it burdened him to hear this fatalism creep into her outlook on life, especially since it threatened the raw energy of youthful conviction that had nourished his humanity over the past two weeks.

"You're right," he said. "You're right about all of this stuff. But listen to yourself. It sounds to me like you want to go down in a blaze of glory, telling the world to go fuck itself and then afterwards remain silent and waste away here. It's not as black and white as that, though. You'll have tons of other chances to get out of here and tons of other chances to be heard—if you actually pursue them. I mean, look, I chose to waste away here and I really regret that. When I watched that movie you showed me, that's what I thought.

Regret. Tons of fucking regret for burying my head in the sand and waiting it out here. Yeah, I could have gone somewhere else and been equally as fucked, but at least I wouldn't be living in a dying town, being slowly poisoned by the water."

"Which proves my point," she said, "it is impossible to get away from here. This place'll drag you down with it."

"No," said Randy, "what it proves is that, if you give up while you're young and stay here, things will go to shit. It proves that you should get out while you can. What's the point of hating the system if you just bow down to it in the end?"

Blake exhaled through her teeth in what sounded like a combination of a sigh and a giggle.

"At least you didn't say 'you're only 20' or 'time will tell' or some bullshit like that," she said with a smirk, resting her head on his chest. "So what happened to you? How did you wind up here? You don't look great…like you've been through some hard shit or something."

Randy cautiously caressed the hair on the side of her face again and, seeing that she didn't pull away, took the risk of placing a light kiss on the back of her head.

"Well, when the riot police came onto the scene, everyone ran in a million different directions and I ran into this group of cops. They cuffed me. I spent a few days in jail and I was transferred here for 'rehabilitation.' Apparently, I have to show them I can socialize and have some job skills and they'll let me go."

Blake laughed.

"Yeah, I have to finish out the semester here, keep a B average and then they'll send me home. They've got me cleaning the bathrooms and collecting the trash for my 'job skills' training. They're so fucking serious about it that I couldn't even leave this floor until yesterday. Guess they figure this is where a sociology degree will land me."

"I'm just doing what they're asking me to do and not complaining too much. I just want to get the fuck out of here as soon as possible," said Randy.

"At least you can work your way out," she said. "No flexibility for me. I've got to just study and clean and wait for my transcript to get sent here."

"When does your semester end?" asked Randy

"Three and a half weeks from now. The professors have been good about letting me work from here though."

They talked for hours until the sun began to set. The strange, sterile aura of Oakvale seemed to transfigure the world around them, as if they now occupied some secret space that resisted the forces of time and circumstance that would otherwise pull them apart. The topics moved from their childhood, to school, to their first loves, to politics, to pop culture and art. It was the kind of honest, open conversation that Randy hadn't experienced since he was in his twenties, and he wished to linger in these forgotten pleasures of unstructured, heartfelt interaction.

When they heard some of the orderlies gathering supplies in the closet next to the recreation room, they got up and walked through the hallway, with Blake holding Randy's finger and guiding him towards her room, which was on the other end of the floor. As they stood in the doorway, Blake leaned in, kissed him softly on the lips, and gave him a probing, passionate look that paralyzed him with nervousness. It was a look that he had seen before in different situations with different women. It was an expression that seemed to communicate something like, "I'm ready. Your move," and it would always disarm him to the point of inaction, of questioning whether his "move" would be the right one and worrying if the hairy, asymmetrical plainness of his body would disgust his partners. Tonight, however, the concern wasn't so much the plainness of his appearance as it was the deterioration of his body. He thought about the image that he encountered in the bathroom mirror on the night of his arrival–the face of a balding, blotchy-skinned middle-aged man whose physique was caught in a state of gradual atrophy. Unlike in past circumstances, however, he was motivated to pursue his desires by a powerful physical attraction and a deep emotional admiration for Blake, which he had never felt before; and, while his body was in a state of overall decline, he possessed an unnaturally strong erection, as if some uncontrollable, youthful energy was trying to break free from the shackles of age and illness that plagued him.

He grabbed her waist and pressed her body against his, kissing her deeply and fully with his tongue. He then stopped to kiss the soft skin under her neck, which had a radiant warmth despite its appearance of pallor. He closed the door behind him and walked her back into the room, guiding her with his hands still on her hips until they reached her bed, which was a small hospital bed with a railing stuck in its upright position. Randy tried to push it down and it eventually broke off and fell to the floor, which made them pause, giggle, and listen to see if anyone was coming to check on the room.

After a few moments of silence which confirmed their privacy, Randy sat her down and leaned into kiss her, bracing her head with his hands. Blake ended the kiss with a broad smile and pushed him away as she leaned back and stared at him.

"Take your clothes off," she said.

Randy stood there for a moment, worried that this was the point at which he would be exposed for having a sickly, repulsive body. Male nakedness, he thought, was always off-putting in the stark immediacy of direct observation, but he knew that he was too old to allow shyness and insecurity to deny him this moment, so he stripped off his shirt and slacks and, with a lump in his throat, removed his undershirt, socks and boxers. He stood there in silence, trying to look away, but felt a throbbing eagerness between his thighs that both surprised and embarrassed him.

"Come here," said Blake, pulling him towards her until she could put her arms around his back and hug him. As she began to kiss his stomach and chest, he could feel his penis pressing into her warm body. Her hands caressed his lower back, after which she flipped her wrists over and ran the tips of her nails over his buttocks and lower thighs, causing goose bumps to rise up and cover his body.

She then stood up and took hold of his penis, squeezing and stroking it as she leaned in to kiss him. The first kiss was long and passionate, but the second and third were more playful, as she pulled her lips away sooner and sooner and beckoned Randy to chase her. She eventually made no contact at all and, giving him a seductive smile, dropped to her knees and tossed her hair back as she brought his penis to her mouth. She took him in just at the tip, sucking lightly and flicking at him with her tongue. It had been so long since Randy felt such sensations of pure pleasure that, with his heart jumping from beat to beat, he feared ruining the moment with a premature reaction. There was also something strangely anticlimactic about defaulting to a blowjob, as if he was giving himself over to a juvenile impulse that could rob this encounter of its potential significance.

He pulled back.

"What's wrong?" asked Blake in a whisper.

"Nothing. Nothing." said Randy.

He grabbed her under her arms and coaxed her to stand up. He removed her t-shirt and kissed the base of her neck as he eased her back towards the bed. They sat down together and he clutched her large, supple breasts in his hands and massaged them as he again kissed her chapped lips. He leaned her back and, with her legs dangling off the edge of the bed, removed her pajama bottoms and slid his arm under her legs to move her into a more secure position. He looked down in awe at her near naked body, which had voluptuous curves that were always hidden by her oversized clothes. Though reclined, her breasts remained firm and her nipples stood erect in the excitement of the moment. Her stomach was small and soft, its youthful beauty interrupted somewhat by a large, scaly red rash that stretched from just under her navel to her upper thigh. Her legs were long, firm, and smooth, although there were similar rashes visible on her calves and ankles. But what fascinated him the most was the space between the top of her thigh and her buttocks— a small, v-shaped divot where her legs ended and her rear began. It seemed, so he thought, that there was always one singular, isolated point on a woman's body that both connected it to the universal beauty of the female form and yet lent every woman a thrilling uniqueness that caused an almost sublime pain in a lover sensitive enough to appreciate it. It was a realization he had come to long ago, but that had receded from his memory as his existence grew lonelier and more isolated. In rediscovering it now, he found himself trapped in motionless adoration.

"I know," said Blake, blushing and covering the rash on her waist, "it's pretty disgusting, but they say it's not contagious."

Randy's reverie was broken for a moment, and it took him a few seconds to realize what she was talking about.

"You're so beautiful," he whispered. "I wouldn't change any inch of you."

He leaned over on the bed and placed a kiss just below her navel while, at the same time, slipping his fingers under her thong and sliding it down her legs. He kissed her knees, her inner thighs, and the base of her vagina, which caused her to shiver with excitement. He then proceeded to kiss his way up her body, ending at her lips, at which point he parted her legs with his and entered her. Her body was eager and wet and Randy focused on increasing the intensity of his movement to please her as best he could, while not giving himself over to the ripples of pleasure that were moving through him. He could feel her tremble as she came, and he rolled over beside her and held her in his arms.

"Thank you," he said, kissing her on the forehead.

"No," she said, "thank you."

Randy smiled.

Blake looked at him with a dazed sense of satisfaction, running her fingers up and down his chest.

"I think you're the first person who's ever called me beautiful," she said.

"Nonsense," said Randy, his still quickened pulse interfering with his breathing.

"It's true."

"I bet lots of guys have called you beautiful."

"They've called me things. Doable. Slutty. Hot. That stuff, mostly. I'd rather be beautiful," she said, rolling on top of him.

"Well, you're one of the most beautiful women I've ever seen. I just don't get why you would even talk to someone like me."

"Because you're nice. I could tell that you were nice even though you were quiet and..." she paused to laugh, "kind of old and nerdy."

She gave him a peck on the lips and looked into his eyes to see if he was offended by the comment. Randy didn't quite know how to respond without resorting to some form of self-deprecation, which didn't seem to fit the moment, so he stayed silent and kissed her back.

"And when I told you about the protest. You were nervous, but you didn't immediately get mad or call me crazy. That meant so much to me," she said, beginning to caress the side of his body from his ribs to his thighs. "This is so silly, but before Jay I had this boyfriend. I was really young and he was much older than me—and I was bothering him to come with me on this nature hike thing my youth group had organized. And I know it was dumb, but I was really into it and I kept on pestering him and eventually he got angry and said 'Just drop it, you stupid cunt.' And like, it really hurt and I don't think I really knew what that word meant and it hurt. And Jay is like that too. Not really mean about things like that guy, just kind of small-minded and irritable. But you just listened. You didn't judge. You didn't snap. I mean, fuck, you got arrested because of me and you don't seem that mad!"

"Come on, you're amazing. I don't regret a second of it. Guys would do anything to be with a person like you," said Randy, still partially aroused but fighting sleep.

"Uh, not exactly," she said, snickering, "I hate to call you old again, but I don't think you realize what it's like now with dating and relationships and stuff. Guys ignore you. It's hard to find a time to meet up, especially if they have a max hour gig, and when you do meet up, it's just for a quick hook up or something.

And people are really intolerant, too. If you even bring something up that's, like, not in their comfort zone to talk about, they get all pissy."

Randy could feel her hand exploring the crease of his thighs and felt his body responding. There was so much more he wanted to say to her. His choking episode was weighing on him and he wanted desperately to tell her about it, to express his uncertainties about his health and the fear for the future that had been gnawing at him for the past few weeks, but he decided against it. He didn't want to infect the evening with his fears and paranoias. He simply wanted to enjoy the privilege of being in her presence and hoped that the moment would last indefinitely, so he gripped her buttocks and held her as she rubbed against his body.

"Can we try something?" she asked, pressing her hands against his chest and sitting upright.

"Yeah."

She shifted her weigh to one side and lowered herself onto him, closing her eyes as if to find the right position by sensation alone. She moved with caution and uncertainty at first, savoring what appeared to be a new form of pleasure for her. She glanced down at Randy and, seeing that he was blissfully absorbed in feeling the subtleties within her, gave him a look of anticipatory excitement. She began to move more freely and vigorously, the force of her body shaking the bed as she thrust her head back and surrendered them both to an intense, liberating orgasm.

RANDY AND BLAKE WERE AWOKEN the next morning by a friendly but persistent knock from an Oakvale staff member. When the two did not immediately respond, the woman cracked opened the door and peaked her head in.

"Breakfast is only until 10," she said with a smile.

"Ok, thank you," said Blake with restrained irritation.

"Oh, and Mr. James, you have an appointment scheduled today with Dr. Ross. Please meet him at eleven in Mr. Jiminez' office," added the woman.

Randy grunted in response and wondered how this woman, whom he had never seen before, knew who he was and what he was scheduled to do.

"What's that about?" asked Blake, rolling over on to Randy's chest and gazing at him with a broad, sleepy smile.

"Not sure," said Randy, "I had a check-up of sorts when I got here, probably just about that."

He thought again about telling her the truth, but the melancholy of imminent departure after a night of bliss was its own unique sadness that demanded his complete attention. The experience of time, he thought, was quite strange. Their night together was so emotionally nuanced and satisfying that each individual moment seemed to stretch out and fill an incalculable expanse of time and yet, now that the morning had come, everything felt unfairly brief and ethereal. It seemed, in hindsight, that his ten years of increasing loneliness and romantic alienation were destined to end in her embrace, but now that the moment had passed, he was stung by the impossibility of their situation. The uncertainty of what would happen next muted his ability to express what he wanted to say to her— an insistent sentiment that existed somewhere between reverence and love.

"What do we do?" he asked, kissing her on the forehead.

Blake rolled over onto her back and stared at the ceiling.

"I have no fucking idea," she said.

"What do you want to happen?" asked Randy

"I want to be with you. I want to get the fuck out of this hell hole. I want to be true to Jay. I want to live my life without wondering when this shit is going to consume me. It all seems basically impossible."

"I know," said Randy.

"I've just been with Jay for so long, you know. I feel like I can't hurt him, but I don't want to hurt you. This is all so fucked up."

"Do you regret what happened?"

"No. I just regret that we didn't meet sooner," she said with a helpless smile. "And I'm also really sorry for all this. I mean, you're stuck here because of me. You got arrested and I didn't even make it to the protest. Then we get here and…this happens and I feel like it will really fuck with our minds. But I don't regret it."

"I don't want you to be sorry for anything," said Randy, feeling a flutter in his chest. "The fact is I've spent my life waiting for something. Just sitting around waiting for something to happen. Waiting to do *something*. Without you, I'd still be waiting."

"Please don't stop talking to me," Blake said.

"Never," he said.

Randy got up, searched for his clothes on the floor, and began getting dressed. Blake did the same. They walked hand in hand to the door, paused, and stared into each other's eyes is if to confirm that last night wasn't an aberration. Randy drew Blake towards him and they kissed, lingering in a passionate embrace that sought desperately to delay the inevitable pull of time that was separating them.

Randy then forced himself to leave. Walking down the hall to the elevator, he felt as if he were in a tunnel that brought the hopelessness of his situation into focus. He knew that there was no future for he and Blake and that, even if she did leave Jay and decide to be with him, he could offer her no tangibly better future than his friend. He could, of course, try to sell his house and move away from the Corridor with her, but there was no housing market left in the city. The best he could hope for would be to sell it off to a local resident for a grand or two, who would then hold onto it to collect the monthly profit sharing payment until the property fell into complete disrepair. And even if they just left, there was no guarantee that they could find work in any of the major cities that still had thriving economies, which, in any case, often had residency laws that restricted the ability of unemployed people to move into their jurisdictions. He also knew that he would feel guilty for pulling Blake into the spiral of stagnation and fading opportunity that his life had become and, no matter how much she protested to the contrary, Randy believed that she still had a real hope of avoiding the fate that life in the Corridor foisted upon people.

Randy entered Carlos' office still lost in these considerations. He sat down, stared blankly at his phone and, shortly thereafter, a balding doctor with a wrinkled, exhausted face entered the room and sat down beside him.

"Hello Mr. James," said the doctor, extending his hand, "I'm Dr. Ross and I'm here to talk about the films we obtained from you two days ago."

Carlos began taking notes.

"You had an episode of choking," the doctor continued, "which led to a period of unconsciousness, at which point I ordered a CT scan of your chest and abdomen to determine if there were conditions or mechanical obstructions that would cause such a reaction. What we found was a large mass in the esophagus that is likely obstructing your ability to swallow whole foods effectively. Now, your esophagus is not completely blocked, but this condition typically leads to severe discomfort, which might be causing a kind of post-prandial anaphylactic reaction which intensifies your symptoms and leads to a sensation of choking. This would be consistent with several other smaller, open lesions we found in your throat that have probably been made worse by your persistent coughing and retching and could account for the blood you brought up during the incident. Any questions?"

Randy was silent for a minute as he tried to clear his mind from thoughts of Blake and focus on the information he had been given.

"Mass?" he asked. "Like cancer?"

"It is very likely a malignancy," the doctor replied. "That would be consistent with its size and location. Now, if you were to go get it staged at a facility specializing in oncologic care, I suspect they would say it is somewhere between a stage 3 and 4."

Carlos continued taking notes.

"So what can I do about it?" asked Randy, with pronounced panic and anger in his voice.

"Well, based on my discussions with Mr. Jiminez about your insurance coverage and overall financial situation, I think that an aggressive intervention is unlikely, so I recommend an adaptive, palliative approach to maintain nutrition levels and manage anxiety and emergent pain. I am going to give you two prescriptions. The first is a medication called Lorezapem, which should help reduce your anaphylactic reactions. I am also going to prescribe something called Fentanyl, which will help with pain. You can start getting it in pill form and then switch to a suspension or a lollipop variety if and when you find it difficult to swallow. I also recommend slowly moving to a liquid diet to maintain your strength. Any type of protein shake will be fine. Good luck to you."

The doctor stood up and shook Randy's hand before he could ask any further questions, then left the room with a quick, authoritative stride. Randy kicked the door closed behind him.

"So you guys give me a fucking death sentence like it's nothing!" Randy screamed.

Carlos smiled.

"Come on, Randy. Negativity is not going to help this situation. We gave you a proactive care plan and if you get your finances in order, it's not out of the question to head to a facility better capable of managing your condition. There are some great new therapies out there that can really help you."

Randy laughed and leaned closer to Carlos.

"Do you guys believe your own bullshit or do you laugh about fucking with people in the break room? I might actually have more respect for you if you treated this shit like a gag," he said, somewhat impressed at the way his terminal diagnosis made him feel liberated enough to say what came to his mind.

"Randy, why regress now?" said Carlos, "You've made such progress in the short time you've been with us. Your performance in the work program has been excellent, you've become more social, and you've overcome your fear of intimacy. It's all been really positive."

"Fuck is that supposed to mean!" said Randy, rising from his chair.

"Please sit down. Rage will not help you," said Carlos.

"I've been diagnosed with fucking cancer!"

"You've been made aware of a potentially unfavorable health outcome. Now it is up to you to manage it as the doctor instructed. You have a plan in place and, like I said, you have the option of pursuing new treatments at other facilities."

"Oh man...you're fucking pathetic. Fuck this."

Randy got up to leave, slamming the chair against the desk.

"Randy," said Carlos assertively, "We are discharging you today. Please stay here and do not rejoin the population. A staff member will bring you your things."

Carlos tapped a code into his cell phone, which immediately resulted in two armed guards entering the room and standing near the door.

"So you guys send people away to die? Should have assumed as much. Even though I hate this place and I'd rather drop dead anywhere else," said Randy.

"Totally incorrect," said Carlos. "Your care plan can be managed independently. If you need some input from us, we're always on call."

A nurse entered the room and handed Randy a bag with his belongings, brochures about his condition, and a three-month supply of the medications the doctor had prescribed. The guards escorted him to the main entrance of the building and blocked the doorway in case he tried to re-enter. When Randy inquired about the possibility of getting a ride to his car, they informed him that no vehicles were available, leaving him to make the frigid, three mile walk on his own.

The city was bathed in an austere sunlight which seemed more appropriate to mid-winter and created a mix of light and shadow that brought the abandoned houses and shops into sharp relief. The roads were so empty and still that the only sounds audible to Randy were those made by his sneakers slapping against the pavement and the call of birds in the distance. Sadness, anger, hate, hopelessness, acceptance and love flowed through his mind in contemplative dissonance.

166

12

Randy's house was just as he had left it. The dishes in the sink sat in a pool of now rancid water, his bed was unmade, and the used cups on the bathroom floor displayed lip marks of dried blood. Over the past few years, he had spent fewer and fewer hours in the house itself, preferring instead the confines of the game room as his main living quarters, entering the house only to sleep. Today, however, he walked through each room, allowing himself to feel the sting of lingering memories, which hung in the air like the slowly dissipating smoke of a past not fully faded from the world.

He ended his tour in the TV room, where he had found his father's body sixteen years ago. Though his face had been severely disfigured by the blast of his gun, his father had retained a familiarity in the onset of death. His expression, while by no means peaceful, maintained an uncanny naturalness, as if frozen in the act of contemplating the ultimate consequences of what he had done. This same familiarity of expression was evident on his mother's face as well, when, standing in the hospital to identify her body, Randy remembered deceiving himself into thinking that she was simply asleep–that the cold paleness of death could be chased away with a nudge on the shoulder and a whisper that would call her back into existence. He wondered what the final expression on his face would be and who would be there to see it. Perhaps, he thought, it would be better to just die and not worry about such considerations.

Force of habit brought him to the game room. Its curated order and tightly-packed shelves now seemed foreign to him, a product of his planning that he had not noticed before. He had spent so many hours in the room, expended so much time, effort and money obsessively searching for and assembling its individual prizes that he neglected to appreciate the entirety of its appearance, which was at once a museum of gaming history and a monument to his past. For sixteen years, he had methodically expanded his collection, system by system and game by game. Some games were nostalgic icons of his childhood. Others were rare gems whose scarcity alone made the process of acquisition its own unique pleasure, placing him in the role of a treasure hunter, rummaging around the outskirts of the Corridor to cherry pick the last vestiges of digital leisure from yard sales, charity auctions, Goodwill stores, and abandoned homes and warehouses. This thrill of the hunt, combined with a near constant surveying of auction sites and Internet forums, allowed weeks to fade into months and years, and each individual system and game to become a signpost of sorts, according to which the passage of time could be measured.

Randy always took a certain pride in meandering the shelves of the game room and recalling how he came into possession of each piece of hardware and software and what it meant in the context of his personal history and the history of gaming. He felt an almost exquisite pleasure in sitting down with a beer and playing *Street Fighter Zero 3* on the Sega Saturn, knowing that he was only one of a handful of people left in the region who both owned it and could appreciate its technical mastery and historical significance. He handled his boxed copy of *Earthbound* with near reverence, playing it once a year with ever greater admiration for its riffs on a suburban America that no longer existed. He took pride in playing through *Snatcher* on his JVC X'Eye, for which he had paid three months' worth of salary without the slightest hint of hesitation. Even though there was no one in his life who could truly appreciate what he had accomplished as a collector, he never felt the need to communicate the passion of his pursuits beyond a small community of Internet enthusiasts, from whom he received enough recognition and encouragement to continue expanding his collection.

Being diagnosed with cancer, however, and knowing that he was about to die, even without knowing exactly how long the process would take, made him look at these walls with regret. The history which inhered in each game now seemed meaningless, and the objects themselves nothing more than small specks of plastic and silicon in a mosaic of wasted opportunity. When life is measured in an unknown expanse of years, leisure and idleness seem like reasonable pursuits with which to occupy the space between potential and its realization, but when measured in intervals of weeks or months, with the ticking of each second representing a real and measurable process of decline, the remorse of time wasted becomes suffocating. The pain of life ending becomes magnified when that life, in every meaningful sense of the word, never really began. What significance could his collection possibly have when compared to the wealth of human experience that he would be denied? What solace could he possibly take in the scarcity of faded plastic when he could never be with the woman he was beginning to love?

Though the thought of switching on one of these systems pained him, he also began to wonder what the alternative to collecting would have been. Would he feel any different if he had instead sunk his time into some more socially acceptable form of conspicuous consumption? Could any other course of action have had any meaning at all, if it had been undertaken on the periphery of the Corridor? And even if he had finished his master's degree and moved away, he had serious doubts about whether he could have established himself as anything more than an itinerant quasi-professional, who moved from city to city and lived in crowded communal housing while waiting for his chance to land a real, full-time job. Considering that, for so many people—both within and beyond the Corridor—the boundaries separating goals, dreams, and illusions had become virtually indistinguishable, was it so wrong to have clung to a hobby that offered a sense of purpose and a pleasurable escape from an irreversibly damaged life?

Randy sat on the couch, still and silent in the fading light of early evening. He felt a certain irony in that, after a life of continual, if at times subconscious, inaction, it was his inability to act that hurt the most. He was a human spirit trapped in a dying organism and, at the exact moment that a will to agency began burning within him, he had no choice but to wait for his life's inevitable conclusion.

AFTER THREE WEEKS OF LINGERING around his house and his game room in a resigned, depressed stupor, Randy's phone rang. He didn't recognize the number, but answered anyway. It was Blake.

"Hey!" she said with her typical enthusiasm. "I'm out!"

"Great."

"Great? It's awesome! They told me I'm on a watch list or something, but I can go back to school next semester."

"And nothing happened with your phone?" asked Randy.

"Well, they kept it, but I guess if they'd found anything bad I'd still be at Oakvale or worse."

"Probably true," said Randy.

"You sound weird. Are you ok?"

"Just tired, I guess. I miss you, though. Can I see you?" asked Randy.

Blake hesitated.

"I'm at Jay's," she said eventually, "it's, um, kind of hard to… you know."

Randy wanted to tell her to leave, to come be with him and try to be happy, but he knew that very soon the happiness they shared during their moments at Oakvale would be impossible, and it was unfair to ask her to be with him as he died.

"Yeah. I know. Sorry, I, uh, I just…" he said.

"I'm sorry. It's just pretty complicated now."

A painful silence ensued, but neither of them could end the call.

"Look," she said, with a now forced cheerfulness, "Jay is gonna call you. He has this idea about getting that last system you need for the game night."

"I'm not doing that anymore," said Randy.

"Why not?"

"It's a bad idea. No one is going to care about it and it is meaningless now anyway," he said.

"Why is it meaningless now? I thought we all agreed to it," she said.

"I don't know," Randy said, searching for an alternative explanation for his change of heart, "It's just that I'm 38 now and maybe I should stop collecting this stuff. Plus, you guys are really overestimating the interest in gaming. No one out there cares anymore."

"But Jay has already started working on it. He's started creating some buzz on Twitter. And *you* care. This is your thing!"

"Yeah, and what the fuck good has it done me?"

"I don't understand you. Why are you being so negative? You're really depressing me today," she said.

"I don't know. I'm depressed. I'm tired of being...I don't know, I'm just fucking tired of everything," said Randy, repressing an urge to scream.

"Remember what we talked about?" she asked, "about having a voice? About saying something? About just expressing yourself without giving a fuck about who sees it? What happened to that?"

"Yeah," he said, "but I don't know. After all that happened at the protest and jail and Oakvale I just don't feel into it."

"So they win?" she continued, "You are just going to let them silence you? Steal your voice? And this isn't even political or anything. You think they are going to care that you're talking about video games? That's pretty sad."

Randy knew she had a point, but was unsure of how he could find the motivation to care about games.

"I guess you're right, I don't know," he said eventually.

"And I'll be there. I want us all to hang out in the game room, just like we did on the first night I met you."

"Yeah, ok," said Randy, knowing that he could not refuse any offer to be in her presence.

"So here's your assignment," she said, in a playfully authoritative tone, "Talk to Jay and let him help you get that last system you need. Then, when we do the stream, he's gonna handle the tech and I'm gonna film everything. I want you to prepare a little speech or something. We'll start the stream with that. Just talk about what these games and this culture mean to you. Got it?"

"Yeah, sounds good," he said.

"Ok then," she said, trailing off and waiting for him to say something.

Randy remained silent.

"See ya," she said.

The words "I love you" lingered on his tongue and remained there long after he heard the beep of the ended call. Perhaps he had made the wrong decision after all. With death approaching, he wondered, what was the point of withholding his fate from her? The shock and sadness would wear off for her eventually, and he would die without the regret of another missed opportunity. Instead, he had chosen to end his life as he had lived it– trapped in passivity and unable to confront the pressing concerns of his emotional life.

13

Jay arrived to pick Randy up in the early afternoon. They hadn't seen each other in about a month and Randy was surprised to see Jay driving, as he had never mentioned that he had a license or owned a car. He was behind the wheel of a well-maintained 2010 Camaro which, for the Wilkes-Barre area at least, was a quasi-luxury. Randy still did not have a clear idea about where they were going and, although he tried all week to think of a reasonable excuse to back out of the trip, he couldn't think of anything as convincing as the truth about his condition, so he simply remained silent and went along for the ride. He knew only that Jay was going to help him find a Turbo Duo, but Blake was sparse on the details and it seemed unfathomable that Jay could afford or had found this holy grail of the retro collecting scene.

Their interaction was characteristically sparse, but Jay seemed quieter than usual as he navigated the streets of the city and made his way to the Route 81 security checkpoint at a speed bordering on inadvisable. Even on a Saturday afternoon, the checkpoint was busy, with drones scanning every second car and police directing vans and trucks to a weigh station just off the highway. Jay steered the Camaro into the Scranton bypass lane and entered a small service road with signs directing drivers to Route 84, which was one of the last few public roads that led to the state border with New York and New Jersey.

"Where are you going?" asked Randy with surprise.

"Into Jersey," he said.

"You got a road pass?"

"Yeah. Why?"

"Nothing. Just that they're pretty expensive these days," said Randy

"Nah, I got a guy who hooked me up."

Randy hadn't left the state in a decade. Getting a transport pass to move beyond the Corridor cities had become costly and required a sponsorship from a business or government office. Going east was especially difficult, as the New York City metro area states were paranoid about contamination from the Corridor and, unlike Scranton, had no decontamination carwashes or other such protocols for admitting drivers in volume. If they saw a car coming east with Pennsylvania plates, it would be turned back instantly. The fact that Jay had such a pass was significant and, Randy hoped, a sign that they were not on some fool's errand after all.

"So what exactly are we doing?" asked Randy.

"We're getting that Duo, man. Like you said, last piece of the puzzle, right?"

"And how the fuck are we supposed to pay for it?" asked Randy.

"We're not going to pay for it. It's a trade," he said.

"A trade? No one in their right minds would trade a Duo."

"You know that podcaster, Big Jeff?" said Jay. "He would."

Randy was familiar with Big Jeff, but had not followed his work in the last few months. He had the reputation of being a major collector of video games and one of the last widely popular gaming commentators on YouTube. He became famous for videos featuring his over-the-top game room and collection of rare items in a video series called "My INSANE Collection," which captured a sizeable amount of views after the YouTube gaming audience had contracted and other personalities had left the platform due to escalating content creator fees. Big

175

Jeff, it seemed, wasn't bothered by this and invested significantly to enhance his production values, making his work a kind of default destination for whomever was still interested in retro gaming culture.

"Yeah, what about him? What could you possibly trade him that he doesn't already have?" asked Randy.

"I did coding work for him and I'm helping him out with some wiring in his house. And he's paying me with the Turbo Duo."

"He isn't an idiot," said Randy, "Why would he do that when he could just pay you in cash?"

"Dude, you're so fucking uptight" said Jay. "We're going to his place now. I'm going to finish up this work and we're gonna leave with the Duo. Chill and enjoy yourself."

"And Big Jeff invited you over for this?"

"Yeah, he's having another one of those arcade parties and I'm doing this video wall project for him where he can project what is happening on every machine. And then I did this online scoreboard app. It's fucking sick. Everyone who shows up is going to scan in to each machine and their scores will be tallied from game to game and turned into a competition. Dude's giving away some sick prizes too. Don't you listen to his podcast?"

"Not really," said Randy.

"Well, you should," said Jay, "he invited all of his listeners and I offered to do this work for him and we struck a deal. Got us the road pass and everything. Fuckin' sweet."

"Wait," said Randy, "so the guy just said 'Hey, anyone out there listening, come to my house for a party'?"

"Pretty much. The dude's a real fuckin' boss. He stopped chasing console games a long time ago and began buying up old arcade machines and pinballs. I mean, the authentic shit. Real hardware. Not MAME or whatever...No offense."

When Jay approached the New Jersey boarder, New Jersey State Troopers approached in two armored vans and guided them to a checkpoint. An officer came out of a booth and, with a rifle drawn, instructed them to get out of the car. He ushered them to the side of the road and signaled to his staff to scan the Camaro, which they did with a small, handheld device that warbled when in proximity to the tires and the underside of the chassis. The officer kept his gun trained on Jay and demanded his road pass, which he took from Jay's hand and scanned at a barcode reader mounted to a steel post outside of his office. The reader chimed and lit up with three green lights, after which the officer relaxed his gun, gave the pass back to Jay, and told him to have a good weekend.

Once they had crossed the state border, the landscape changed dramatically. The pothole-filled roads and abandoned towns that dotted the Pennsylvania landscape faded away and were replaced with stretches of pristine highway and quaint, well-kept neighborhoods in which life seemed to follow the comforting rhythms of traditional American suburbia. Mothers packed groceries into the back of minivans, customers exited main street storefronts with boutique shopping bags, and people could be seen in the windows of strip mall restaurants enjoying an early dinner. Everyone was well-dressed, every car was only five years old or less and, while there was a police presence on the streets, it was minimal and the officers seemed to enjoy engaging in lighthearted, friendly interactions with residents as they passed by.

Jay and Randy turned off of the main roads and headed for a stretch of smaller country roads that wound their way through vast, wooded hills and ended up in the Sunset Lake region of a town named Sparta. There was no industry or shops of any kind in the area, only immaculately-maintained private residences that stretched out in every direction and were larger than anything Randy had seen since childhood. Even the gated community in which the protest had taken place looked modest compared to the estates that lined the streets around the lake. So often, people in the Corridor cities would talk of getting out and living in some secluded corner of Canada or making the trip to California to buy a small ranch house, which were rumored to still be affordable, but Randy doubted that very few people could even conceive of the kind of wealth, space, and opulence that this community possessed. The distance between Wilkes-Barre and these streets was so vast that both places didn't seem to be of the same world, as if the greatest aspirations and goals of a person like Randy would be incomprehensible to someone who had lived in these surroundings.

Jay parked the car on the end of a cul-de-sac in front of a massive stone house that overlooked the lake. The house gave the impression of being three stone structures that were joined together to create something akin to a castle, were it not for the frequent nods to American McMansion practicality—such as a three car garage, an automatic sprinkler system and some rather plain, white windows—which ultimately rooted the house in the architectural idiom of 21st century conspicuous consumption. It was situated on a slight hill, and as Randy and Jay walked up the winding driveway, they saw a series of bright purple, corrugated cardboard yard signs that pointed them in the direction of the party entrance, which was a storm door to the basement built into the stone foundation of the house.

The doors were open and, having not received a response after shouting "hello" a few times, Randy and Jay descended the steps and found themselves in a finished basement made to look like a classic arcade. There were five rows of meticulously restored arcade machines from the 80s and 90s in the center of the room, with pinball, pachinko, and ski-ball machines along the walls. Just as Jay had described, there was a huge video board hanging from the high ceiling, which could have easily been at home in a college sports arena. The carpets were black with small, florescent-colored specks that gave off a faint glow just as they had in the bowling alleys and movie theater arcades of the past. A glass case with ticket redemption prizes sat off to the corner near the storm door, along with token machines and a stack of plastic swipe cards which were presumably for the contest. This was an obsessive attempt at re-creating an arcade, but there was almost something too perfect about the room, as if it stood more as a monument to disposable income than to the history of American arcade gaming; and yet, with all of the machines turned on, the lights dimmed, and the cheerful cacophony of attract mode music bouncing off the walls, Randy felt a wave of comforting nostalgia that he hadn't experienced since the protest or his time at Oakvale.

Randy and Jay walked toward the front of the arcade, marveling at each of the machines, which were arranged in rough chronological order, when someone called out to them in a booming, baritone voice from a wet bar tucked away in an alcove on the right side of the room.

"You guys here for the party?" he said.

"Yeah," shouted Jay.

The man walked up to them. He was dressed in a tight black Atari T-shirt that seemed custom-made to accentuate his broad shoulders and thick, rippling biceps, but did so at the expense of making visible a wide ring of fat that began at his navel and expanded to his flanks and his back. His body seemed to be that of someone who had access to weight training equipment, but who lacked the discipline to pursue a strict lifting regimen to its completion. He wore tight cargo shorts and a pair of flip flops that were either made in the 80s or were extremely convincing replicas of an 80s brand. He had slicked-back, black hair that receded to the crown of his head and his face had unnaturally smooth skin and an almost porcelain-like sheen.

"Big Jeff, how you guys doin'?" he said, extending his hand to them.

"Hey man, I'm Jay from Pennsylvania and this is my buddy Randy. I'm the guy that made the scoring app you wanted and sent you the wiring harnesses."

"Oh, holy shit," said Jeff, "I didn't recognize your voice in person, man. Thanks for comin.' Everything work out with that road pass?"

"Yup," said Jay, "Cops seemed like assholes at first, but the pass went through."

"They always are, dude. Anyway, you got that app for me?"

"Yeah, it's ready to go," said Jay. "I set up the web server, I just need to get a few test accounts going and we should be up and running."

"Perfect, but we can't do this testing thirsty. Honey!" Jeff yelled, calling up the stairs. "Get the bar going."

His wife entered the basement dressed in black yoga pants and a pink halter top with the Konami code written on the front, the first back-forward inputs of which were lost in her ample cleavage. She seemed to be in her mid-forties and, like her husband, had an athletic build that, upon closer inspection

180

under the lights of the bar, revealed itself to be disproportionate at the waist.

"What can I get you gentlemen?" she asked, reaching under the bar to get three beer glasses with illustrations of popular video game characters painted on them.

"Three Stellas," said Jeff.

She poured the drinks for her husband, who gave her a peck on the lips before serving his guests.

"Fuck, man, you don't look good," he said, giving Randy his beer. "Nothing some draft beer can't cure, though. Am I right?!"

The three walked over to a group of machines and Jeff tested Jay's app, scanning some plastic cards and playing a few rounds of *Pac-man* to see if his scores were being registered. Jay stood by on his laptop, making some tweaks and showing Jeff the backend software that was powering the app and collecting the scores. Randy walked with them, but remained silent, sipping his beer and feeling it sting his chest on the way down. He drank through the pain, however– partly because it no longer mattered, and partly because drinking beer this fresh was a rare luxury.

They proceeded to a row of pinball machines and stopped in front of a working example of the iconic *Twilight Zone* game.

"Here," said Jeff, handing a card to Randy, "you do this test."

"Sure," said Randy, "you don't mind?"

"Nah, man, you need to try this out. Best fucking *Twilight Zone* on the East Coast. It was unsold, factory-fresh stock just sitting around for decades in some guy's warehouse in Virginia. I'm at this point, you know, where I'm just buying these fucking warehouses and storage facilities. I flip the properties and keep the games. That's how I found a lot of this shit. Only way to go these days. Give it a shot."

Randy stepped forward and swiped the card. The game came to life with the sound of Rod Serling's voice and a torrent of blinking, neon lights illuminating the objectives on the play field. He sent the ball coursing along the many chrome ramps and hidden passages with skills that he honed at a local pizza shop when he was a kid, before pinball had made the transition from childhood amusement to adult luxury. *Twilight Zone* was perhaps the pinnacle of the genre– a game of technical intricacy and mechanical refinement, inviting and challenging in a way that few of its counterparts were. It was an elaborate pastiche of America's ludic past; a television show from the 50s, loosely imagined in an amusement of the 70s, with the technical sophistication made available to the genre in the 90s. Big Jeff was probably right in saying that this was the best machine on the East Coast, as the snappiness of the triggers, the sheen of the Mylar play surface and the almost seamless interaction of player and machine felt fresh and new in a way that was only possible with original hardware.

Randy's game came to an end with a frenzied multi-ball session that was too quick for his aging reflexes to manage, and he handed the swipe card back to Jeff.

"Fucking incredible, man" he said.

"Yeah, well, someone's got to keep this shit alive," said Jeff.

Jay and Big Jeff returned to the glass prize counter to look at the results of the test, leaving Randy to wander the arcade for a bit. Jeff's wife sat behind the bar, cleaning glasses and preparing hors d'oeuvres, while knocking back shots at intervals that seemed to follow a pattern known only to her. The room felt alive in anticipation of the guests, as if the machines were

182

eagerly waiting to fulfill the purpose for which they had been built. The pinnacle of the arcade was long gone when Randy was old enough to visit them, but he imagined that this surreal interplay of light and sound—this calm before the storm of people—must have been incredible to witness in the 80s and 90s, when the arcade experience stood as a harbinger for the future of digital amusement.

Guests began arriving within the hour, the majority of them middle-aged couples that seemed to be well-acquainted with Big Jeff and his wife. There were a few teenagers that mixed in with them, as well as some intense looking thirty-somethings who appeared to be scouting the available machines in preparation for the evening's competition. Big Jeff circulated the room and chatted to a few of his friends, leaving Jay to work the prize counter, which seemed to be his designated responsibility for the remainder of the night. The video wall had been activated and was showing a friendly game of *Samurai Showdown*, the score tracking system was up and running, and Big Jeff's wife had managed to get a drink in the hands of everyone who had entered the arcade.

Randy grabbed a swipe card from Jay and began a systematic attempt to play every game in the room, beginning on one side of a row of machines and working his way to the other. He knew it was his last chance to enjoy such a comprehensive overview of arcade history and, since he had been left alone, he relished the opportunity to game in contemplative isolation. According to Jay's stat tracking app, his scores were lagging well behind those who had played the machines before him, but he wasn't concerned with his decline in performance, as he used each machine as a means of reflecting on the past— recollections that, in this lively setting, were insulated from the regret he felt while locked away, alone and dying, in his game room. He played *Space Invaders* with a sense of whimsy at how, upon its release in Japan, it was said to have caused a national shortage of ¥100 coins. He was able to make a one credit run on the original *Street Fighter II* cabinet, which he remembered discovering, neglected, in a dark corner of a movie theater as a teenager. Having been introduced to Street Fighter with the Alpha series, his discovery of an original machine felt like he had unearthed a long-lost treasure—a feeling unique to an era in which gaming and digital amusement had a physical dimension; in which players were forced to navigate the physical world for a few minutes of digital escapism. He teamed up with five other players on a dual screen version of Konami's *X-Men*, a ubiquitous experience of the late 90s arcade scene that had become so rare today that some people in various online arcade forums doubted the existence of working, six player units.

By the time Randy finished his tour, the basement had filled up considerably, to the point that maneuvering around became difficult. Big Jeff and his wife were nowhere to be found, and the guests had now made the bar into a self-serving affair, going through as much beer as possible and now dipping into the multiple bottles of whiskey and vodka that lined a glowing blue shelf behind the taps. Someone had activated the basement sound system and was playing an 80s hit list of sorts, with Billy Ocean's *Caribbean Queen* fading into Phil Collin's *Easy Lover*.

As Randy observed the evolving chaos from the ski-ball corner, which was still more or less unoccupied, he felt a tap on his shoulder. It was Jay.

"Ok, man," he said, barely audible against the din of computerized chirps and pop music, "let's grab that Duo."

"You sure?" asked Randy, "I don't see Dave anywhere."

"Yeah, it's cool with him" shouted Jay, "just follow me."

The two made their way to the stairs leading to the main floor, the door to which had been left open. The steps led to the kitchen, which had become a kind of secondary bar with fifty or sixty bottles of liquor standing, open and half-empty, on a massive granite island in the center of the room. With the kitchen as a staging area, the party had expanded throughout the house. People were smoking on the patio and skinny dipping in the pool, a group of guys ate pizza and watched football on a wall-sized TV in the great room, and several women were giving casual fellatio to their partners on the grand staircase in the foyer.

Jay guided Randy through a series of hallways to a smaller set of stairs at the back of the house, between the garage entrance and the laundry room.

"Ok," Jay said, motioning to Randy, "the game room is this way."

"What the fuck are you doing?" said Randy, "Should you really be sneaking around this guy's place? Just ask him."

"Dude, it's a fucking party. Just roll with it," said Jay.

They went upstairs and walked through a hallway of what seemed like twenty closed doors. Jay was counting them off, as if matching the layout of the hallway to a floor plan he had seen earlier. They stopped at a room on the right side of the hall and Jay pressed his ear to the door in an attempt to detect if it was occupied.

"This is it," he whispered, as he cautiously entered the room.

It was a large bedroom which had been transformed into a video game library. Each wall had specially built shelving that ran floor to ceiling and had rolling library ladders to access the top shelves. The games, all of which were museum quality examples, were carefully stacked on each shelf, some spine-to-spine like books, others fanned outward to show off their uniqueness or rarity. The game systems were kept in glass hobby shop cases in the center of the room, along with various figures and statues from popular video game and comic book series.

Jay walked over to the left end of the case and motioned to Randy. "That's it, isn't it?"

"Fuck," said Randy, shocked to see the illusive black and purple console in person. "There it is."

Jay took out a small crowbar from his backpack and wedged it between the lip of the counter top and the body of the case.

"What the fuck?" said Randy.

"Quiet, dude. Just be fuckin' quiet."

Jay, with the full force of his meager body weight, pressed hard on the end of the crowbar, causing the case to crack open with a loud pop. He then shimmied the crowbar further along the case to disengage more of the hinges, shattering large sections of the glass in the process. He reached into his backpack again, put on a pair of gloves and, after knocking away the remaining shards of glass, eased out the Turbo Duo. On the shelf beneath it was a plastic box labeled "TG16/PC Engine Accessories," but it remained inaccessible through the opening on the top of the case. Jay surveyed the counter and then, seemingly out of haste and frustration, smashed through the glass on the front of the cabinet and took the box from the lower shelf, along with an R. Mika statue that stood next to it, and placed everything in his backpack.

"You go first," said Jay, motioning Randy into the hallway.

"Fuck do I have to go first. You're fucking robbing the guy," said Randy.

" 'Cause you don't have the fucking Duo on you. Give me a signal if you see someone coming and I'll put it back."

Randy walk cautiously into the hallway, with Jay following two steps behind. It was quiet and the doors were closed, except for one on the far end of the hallway near the grand staircase, which had been cracked open, allowing a small blade of light to project into the otherwise darkened space. He noticed that, on both ends of the hallway, there were security cameras mounted near the ceiling. Jay could see Randy pause as he stared up at them and, irritated by the delay, pushed him in the back to continue moving. Randy gave Jay a signal to fall back as he tip-toed toward the opened door. As he passed it, he turned his head and saw Big Jeff having anal sex with a young Hispanic girl, seemingly oblivious to the world around him. Randy turned to Jay, placed his finger over his lips, and the two descended the grand staircase and exited the front door.

THE RIDE BACK TO WILKES-BARRE was equally as silent as the drive into New Jersey. Jay was mildly drunk, which required him to put forth some additional effort to concentrate on the road signs. Randy was feeling a stabbing sensation in his chest that made speaking difficult, forcing him, in as clandestine a manner as possible, to pop a Fentanyl tablet in his mouth and hope that Jay didn't notice.

Over the weeks since his diagnosis, Randy became aware that the opiates prescribed to him no longer gave him a high, but instead allowed him to numb the intense pain that cropped up during certain parts of the day, so that he could maintain a kind of groggy attachment to the rhythms and responsibilities of life. It served as a staunch reminder of the seriousness of his condition which, despite his best efforts to focus on other things, was consuming his body.

He began to wonder why Jay had gone to these lengths to help him complete his collection, why he had robbed a guy with the resources and personality to destroy him, and why he said nothing about Blake, who he assumed had told Jay about what happened at Oakvale. It seemed unreasonable and improbable that Jay would care enough about staging this livestream to take on this kind of personal risk to help a guy who had slept with his girlfriend, especially after seeing a collection like Big Jeff's, which proved that Randy was a small time collector in the broader landscape of the hobby. Jay's enthusiasm for old technology had never made complete sense to him in the past, but tonight seemed out of character—a step over the line separating his gray area business dealings from blatant illegality.

Randy decided to break the silence. "Why did you rip this guy off?"

"Why not?" said Jay, focusing on the road ahead.

"Well, for one, the fucker seems like he has the bankroll to ruin your life," said Randy.

"He won't even know it was me. There weren't any cameras in that game room anyway."

"The hall cameras got us though," said Randy.

"Yeah, but we weren't waving the fucking Duo around," said Jay. "All he can do is assume shit. Plus, I hacked the code to his WiFi and home security system, so I'll play hardball if the fucker wants to play hardball."

Randy leaned back in his seat and saw that they were crossing the Pennsylvania border. There were no security checkpoints heading west.

"Seems like you've grown up a bit, huh?" asked Randy

"Fuck you mean by that?"

"Well," said Randy, "picking a fight with this guy is a little different than helping loners in Wilkes-Barre with off the grid electronics and doing odd jobs around town. This shit could get serious."

Jay looked at Randy with an expression of repulsion and irritation. "This fucker isn't going to do anything. At the end of the day, he's a game collecting nerd and a cheapskate who thought he could get something out of me for free. Nothing's free. And he'll realize that."

Randy was surprised by the hardness in his friend's voice, which was either an aspect of his personality that he had never noticed before or evidence that Jay was developing the zero-sum mentality that was necessary for survival in the Corridor and beyond. Randy was, in a way, proud that his friend possessed audacity to think he could threaten a guy with Big Jeff's resources, but also concerned that, if the confrontation did happen, it could destroy him.

The silence resumed until they reached the outskirts of Scranton, at which point Jay exited the main highway and drove to an old scenic overlook in the hills of the Western Game Lands above the city. The parking lot was old and had been consumed by weeds and overgrown trees, which obscured the once impressive vista of the valley below. Jay parked the Camaro at the far end of the lot, on a patch of blacktop that had not yet been consumed by nature.

"Gimme a half of one of those pills," said Jay, turning and staring at Randy.

Randy broke off a Fentanyl and handed it to Jay, who chewed it quickly and cringed at the bitter taste.

"Get out and follow me."

Jay got out of the car and hopped over a barricade at the edge of the overlook, using his cellphone to guide his steps through the brush. He jaunted forward, as if trying to test Randy and see if he could catch up. The branches of the trees tore into their sweaters and their feet slipped on the undergrowth, which was covered in a glistening, half-frozen dew. They eventually came to a clearing and, before them, was a sprawling view of the northern shale fields, which gave off an iridescent glow of blue and yellow light that climbed toward the sky and masked the existence of the stars. It seemed foreboding and otherworldly, but also strangely beautiful from this distance, with the tips of the drills, the factories, and the skyscraper office complexes losing their individual definition and blending into a kind of metallic organism that seemed to pulsate in the cold, fluttering air of early morning. It was the same view Randy had observed in Blake's video project.

Jay sat down in the grass. Randy joined him.

"Looks fucking different from up here, right?" asked Jay, his speech beginning to slur.

"Yeah."

"Doesn't seemed so fucked up from up here," he said

"I know," said Randy, "it looks cool, like a spaceship or something."

"You ever seen this view before?" asked Jay, glancing at Randy from the corner of his eyes.

Randy paused. "Nah, I didn't even know they let anyone up here anymore."

"True," said Jay, looking back out on the fields, "guess there's nothing left to hunt."

"Still, it's pretty fuckin' peaceful. You can't even feel the drills or anything."

"Might be because we're fucking high. Where'd you fucking get this shit?" asked Jay, his eyes glazing over.

"Let me ask you something," said Randy, hoping to avoid a discussion of his pills and why he had them, "why are you guys helping me with this livestream. I mean, ok, you got the Duo from Jeff and shit, but why not just sell it? Why are you guys so insistent on doing this thing?"

"Why not, dude?"

"Well, for one thing, you saw what a real collector is tonight. I'm just a guy with shit in his garage. No one's gonna come to play what I have and no one's gonna watch."

"Not true," said Jay, "You got heart, at least. Fuckin' Big Jeff just buys all that shit with his bonuses and lords it over the rest of us. Fuck him. You think he knows shit about the Turbo Duo or has even played it?"

"I don't know, man. I just don't think anything I can say about games or show people will matter," said Randy.

Jay threw him an irritated glance. "It means something to Blake. You wanna make her happy at least, right?"

Randy didn't answer and didn't want to probe Jay to figure out exactly what he knew about his relationship with Blake. Jay reached into his jacket, pulled out a cigarette, lit it, and took a long, relaxed drag. He looked back out over the fields and let the smoke pour from his nostrils.

"Now let me ask you something, bro," said Jay, his voice growing more somber, "would you stay here?"

"You mean in Wilkes-Barre?" asked Randy.

"Well, yeah, or in the Corridor in general? I mean, lot's a people say it's the future. They say if you can get a job out there in the fields, you can make a good living. You believe that shit? Or would you leave?"

"Did you get a job offer or something?" asked Randy.

"Nah, man," said Jay, turning to Randy, "I just mean, like, you've been here for a while. You seen some shit. Would you stay or would you go somewhere else? Try to make a new life somewhere?"

Randy saw that Jay had an earnest look in his eyes, as if he was really looking for guidance.

"Jay, man," said Randy, "You've got some major tech skills. If you play your cards right, you could make a decent living here. I'm not going to lie to you about that. But if I were you, I'd get as far away from this place as I could. Fuck this place. And I'd take Blake with you. She doesn't deserve to be trapped here. You guys have too much to live for. Get the fuck out and try to be happy."

"Thanks, man, but what if getting out ain't that easy? I mean, shit, what if it means completely overhauling our lives? Doing stuff we never thought of just to get the chance?"

Randy put his hand on Jay's shoulder and looked him in the eye.

"Do whatever you have to do," he said. "Don't miss your chance."

Jay nodded his head and looked back out at the shale fields as he finished his cigarette. The sun began to rise and its light was starting to reflect off of the tallest buildings on the horizon of the Corridor. Randy and Jay sat there, at first trying to shield their eyes from the glare and then slouching down in the weeds, allowing the comforting numbness of the

Fentanyl and the exhaustion of the previous night to ease them into a nap.

14

Two days had passed, and Randy woke up early in the midst of one of his coughing spells, spitting a thick, maroon mixture of blood and mucous onto his pillow. Since his diagnosis at Oakvale, he began to view these episodes as night terrors rather than unstoppable physical convulsions that signaled the onset of immediate death—a change in perspective that helped him maintain control of his body and, with the help of an Ativan tablet, live out his remaining days as he wished. He walked into the kitchen and contemplated making himself a cheese sandwich, but instead opted for a protein shake and a glass of water, so as not to expend unnecessary energy contracting his throat for an hour to aid in peristalsis. With water in hand, he went outside to observe the bright, cold December morning, cognizant of the fact that, as the days went on, the concept of morning was becoming precious. The experience of finitude made Randy more attentive to the nuances of life he had often neglected—sunlight, laughter, rain, the warmth of his bed, the old man walking a dog on his solitary street. All of these experiences were, of course, clichés that generated nothing more than a reflexive melancholia for the meaningless events and routines soon to be lost, but the certainty of death at an undetermined, but fast approaching point in the future seemed to magnify the banal experiences of life and endow them with a kind of metaphysical significance that Randy, freed from the cynicism and ironic distance with which he used to approach the world, was quick to embrace. When things no longer matter, he thought, sentimentality is permissible.

He made his way from the driveway into the game room, switched on the large space heater near his couch and huddled in front of it, draped in a blanket, waiting for the chill of the space to dissipate. Tonight was the gaming history stream, and Blake and Jay were coming over at seven to help set up. Randy had received texts of encouragement from Blake, urging him to come up with a script for his introduction and little blurbs about each system and game he was displaying. Jay's plan was to embed his commentary into the stream itself, so that viewers could click on a button within a particular video feed and get some background information on what they were watching. After the stream ended, Blake was going to edit the footage down to an hour, add in his intro, and upload it as a video project to YouTube, which viewers could pay a dollar to view. Were his attention not diverted to the brutal seriousness of his own circumstances, he would have been excited about the idea. Back in his "content creator" phase, when he blogged about collecting and posted the occasional collection update video online, he might have even purchased the equipment to do one of these streams on his own. Ten years after the mainstream appeal of retro culture, however, it was likely a wasted effort, and the only thing motivating him even to enter the game room and plan for the night was the chance to spend more time with Blake, even though he knew this romantic instinct was ultimately meaningless.

The key problem for Randy in planning his introductory video was identifying what to say about video games that hadn't already been said. Standing in front of his shelves and talking about the history of games was a pointless gesture, as even a cursory search of the YouTube archives would reveal thousands of similar videos that had become irrelevant to contemporary audiences. He thought about perhaps discussing his personal history as a collector, but then decided that his autobiography was hardly worth committing to video. Few people, he thought, wanted to hear the story of how he spent the majority of his adult life amassing a collection of games in a garage while his town and his body were deteriorating. He also couldn't sell himself on the higher brow, "video games as art" arguments that had circulated around the Internet for the better part of a decade, as he always felt silly defining his love for *Sonic the Hedgehog* or *Mega Man* as examples of a connoisseur sensibility. Randy had very little insight into what art was, nor did he ever care to pursue the subject, but he looked at people who analyzed issues of "ludonarrative dissonance" in the *Uncharted* series and the sexual politics of virtualized gender fluidity in *Skyrim* as pseudo-intellectual dilettantes who sought to appropriate games for their own purposes. He didn't devote his life to games because they represented some greater artistic truth, but he nonetheless was never able to articulate, with any level of analytical refinement, why they were important to him.

After Oakvale, he even found himself unconvinced by his previous belief in the power of gaming nostalgia. Nostalgia felt like a meaningless illusion that he had gleefully constructed for himself in order to ignore the realities of a life that he secretly detested. In his state of increasing pessimism, he was no longer convinced that games possessed the ability to erase the barriers between past and present. This idea seemed to be nothing more than a personal prejudice that neglected the cultural afterlife of any number of products that people once enjoyed—from films, to TV, fashion, cars— even designer towns had sprung up to resemble different periods in American consumer history. In truth, nostalgia had become an industry unto itself, and gaming nostalgia only maintained the veneer of authenticity because it was still curated by an independent fanbase rather than the country's entertainment conglomerates, who believed its appeal was too small to warrant extensive investment.

The benefit of hindsight also made games seem rather suspicious in their intentions, particularly in an era when game creation had morphed into gamifcation, which had less to do with video games as such, and was instead integrated into larger networked platforms as a means of shaping, manipulating, and tracking human behavior. Video games, it seemed to Randy, always had this latent potential to manipulate and deceive—to present a pre-defined set of possible actions and their outcomes as an exercise in player choice and freedom. Whether it was early examples of the medium like *Mario* or the *Legend of Zelda*, or the most recent VR games, which immersed players in worlds of unfathomable graphical and spatial detail, games were, at their core, a visual medium through which people structured and controlled the actions of others. It was, perhaps, telling that when the curtain was pulled back a bit and this reality was exposed to the world—such as in the Blizzard scandal of 2019, which revealed that the developer was analyzing player choices, decision strategies, and speed of input and selling this data to insurance companies and corporations to aid in risk assessment and employment decisions—gamers simply accepted this as one more instance of the invisible background surveillance to which everyone assents. As games moved from consoles to smartphones, the prevailing attitude became one of "if you play well, you have nothing to worry about." Video games had thus lost their character as an oasis of pleasure in the stifling continuum of personal and professional obligation, and had become instead a proving ground for the clever, the obsessive, and the dexterous on which to increase their share of human capital.

Randy began to pace around the room. None of these reflections were useful to the task at hand and, at any rate, he didn't want his pessimism to spoil what was sure to be one of his final interactions with Blake. She and Jay, in spite of everything that had happened, were still enthusiastic enough about the idea to invest the time and money to bring the project to completion, so a short and banal statement would be preferable to one of resentment and splenetic despair. It wouldn't be what Blake had envisioned, but it would at least mask the reality of a sick, lonely man spending the remainder of his days regretting a life of self-imposed inertia.

He circled back to the couch and decided to hook up the Turbo Duo, which had been sitting on the shelf below the entertainment center since Jay had procured it for him. He popped in his favorite title, *Blazing Lasers,* which softened his mood a bit and allowed him to appreciate the beauty of the system.

The console was an example of impeccable, if understated industrial design, with smooth edges and purple lettering that perfectly accented its nineties-style black plastic shell. The controller had a simple elegance, with two buttons, a D-pad, and a pair of notched turbo switches all resting in a housing of textured plastic with a smooth insert around the buttons. Turning the console around, it was clear that it had been modified with component terminals, which probably meant that it also had new capacitors, making it a unique example that cost an astronomical amount of money.

Though Randy had not owned the system before, he did manage to collect a stack of games for it, which he ran in emulation on a computer for the better part of two decades. The software came on two types of media–a credit card sized plastic chip, termed a HuCard, that was inserted into the machine like an ATM card, and a CD-ROM. This combination gave the system a futuristic aura back in the early-to-mid 90s, especially since competing systems could not offer this technology in a single unit. The hardware had a few different iterations prior to the release of the Duo, but there was something about this particular implementation that seemed to complete the promise of the system, even though it was released in the twilight of its lifecycle in North America. It was a classic example of a machine that was neglected in its own time, but whose brilliance could only be appreciated in hindsight. It was a brilliance that began to cut through Randy's despair and remind him of the happier days of collecting, when finding and restoring this console would have been a momentous accomplishment.

It wasn't, however, purely the hardware, the design, or even the software that made the Duo so alluring, but rather the fact that it represented a kind of inflection point in the history of gaming. Though not widely popular in North America, it was a dominant presence in the Japanese market during its lifespan, where it was known as the PC-Engine and was home to a prodigious burst of creativity in the Japanese gaming scene (and any self-respecting foreign collector would, without question, have the necessary adapters to bypass its region-locking and access this wealth of exclusive games). Its combination of enhanced graphics and CD storage allowed developers to create games that, for the first time, closely mirrored the culture out of which they emerged, and this culture of late 80s and early 90s Japan was one that was beginning to explore issues of economic decline, digital escapism, and the tension between the promise and dangers of technological progress. While the games never dealt with these issues overtly, and the properties on which these games were based were usually sci-fi cartoons or comic strips, the system nonetheless offered a glimpse into a society that had created numerous early examples of virtualized worlds which seemed to presage the more severe cultural and social circumstances that much of the West came to inhabit. It did so while remaining rooted in the paradigm of pleasurable human-machine interaction and lighthearted escapism, but it was, for many collectors, these cheerful nods to a dystopian future that made the system and its games so popular over the past decade, whether as a compensatory diversion or a darkly comedic alternate history.

Randy counted himself among those who took a perverse pleasure in comparing the 2020s that he knew to the 2020s imagined by Japanese manga artists, animators, and video game programmers. There were no robots, space voyages, mega cities, cyborgs, or neural implants—and certainly no room for heroic human beings to bend technology to their will in epic battles or spectacular insurgencies. The 2020s, for him, was a time of mass exodus from the city, a time of rapid expansion in the shale fields, and a time during which the bundle of mutated cells in his chest slowly began growing into the painful lump that was now choking the life from his body.

BLAKE AND JAY CAME OVER in the early evening and began setting up video capture equipment. Jay linked three systems per capture card, which involved excavating a mess of tangled wires from behind the circular shelf and routing everything from there to a control hub and a laptop he had set up in the center of the room. Blake created a small studio space in front of Randy's game shelves in order to record his intro and descriptions of the various game systems. It was the ubiquitous background shot of almost all gaming content on YouTube for the past 20 years and, as desperately as he wanted to avoid it, he remained silent and made some notes on the various systems he would describe. Webcams were set-up on the far side of the room to capture people playing the arcade cabinet, the Virtual Boy, and the Vectrex—an old, exotic, and long-forgotten console that displayed games in vibrant, vector-based graphics on a built-in tube TV.

With all of the equipment crammed into the room, it became hard to move around without tripping over wires or bumping into tripods, and Randy was thus relieved when he discovered that Blake and Jay found very few people who agreed to show up. A friend of Jay's from one of his tech support gigs stopped by and was helping with the wiring and signal tests and two of Blake's friends from college who also lived in Wilkes-Barre were supposed to come by later in the evening. There had never been more than 4 people in the game room at one time and Randy felt relieved to know that he didn't have to play the role of host and security guard to a large gathering of people.

As the four worked to setup the room, Randy found himself glancing at Blake, hoping that perhaps a quiet, unspoken acknowledgment of his gaze would be enough for her to excuse herself to have a smoke or take a trip into the house, which could have led to a few precious moments of private conversation and a chance for Randy to say goodbye. Blake did acknowledge him, but only with a look that communicated the impossibility of their circumstances, after which she returned to casual conversations and a few flirty interactions with Jay. It was painful for Randy to see her peck Jay on the cheek as they sat together testing the video feeds or wrap her hands around his waist and kiss his back as he followed specific wires on the ground to their connection points. It was clear that she had made her choice and, whether it was out of habit, loyalty, or hopelessness, it was apparent that their time together at Oakvale would be nothing more than a moving interlude to the separate and inescapable paths their lives were taking.

Jay made some final adjustments to the capture equipment and then asked Randy to turn on all of the systems in the entertainment center.

"See," he said, handing Randy the laptop, "each game is embedded in the feed. Just click on one and it will go full screen."

The stream was a single video player divided up into three rows of four clickable tiles, each showing the feed from a separate system in the room. Viewers would simply have to click on the tile in which they were interested and could then watch whatever was being played in full-screen mode. A small icon shaped like an NES controller on the lower left-hand corner of the screen functioned as a home button, which would return users to the tile layout to select a new game, and a clickable smiley face icon next to it would launch a popup showing Randy's brief historical commentary in a picture-in-picture mode. It was an elegant interface and, if they actually had enough people to play all of the systems at once, it would have offered a comprehensive survey of the sliver of gaming history preserved in Randy's garage. As it stood, however, only six different systems would be featured at a time, with the rest of the consoles running demo modes for their respective games.

Blake motioned to Randy.

"Let's do the system descriptions," she said.

Randy sat down in front of his game shelves with his note cards in hand. He was nervous and noticeably agitated, as he had not appeared on video since his mid-twenties and had become reluctant to show his face on any online platform. Now, however, that such long term security considerations were meaningless, he plodded through each card in chronological order, offering release dates, system specs, and a brief synopsis on the games being played. His voice was flat and uninspired, and, with each sentence he spoke, he struggled to suppress a dry, violent cough that was building within him. He was immersed in the hobby that he loved, in the company of a woman who had, during their brief time together, changed his life, and yet he couldn't summon the slightest hint of energy to project to the camera.

Blake noticed the dullness and hesitancy of his delivery and was mildly upset.

"What's wrong with you?" she asked

"I don't know," said Randy. "Nervous, I guess."

"Come on," she said, with a perplexed smile, "what's there to be nervous about?"

"I'm not really an on-camera personality."

"Who said you were a personality?" asked Blake, giggling. "Think of yourself as a teacher. As an expert. As someone who's gonna show the world all of this incredible stuff you've got in this room."

"An expert?" said Randy, "An expert in stuff no one gives a shit about."

"Fuck," said Blake, "You're such a downer tonight. Have a few drinks or something."

Jay walked over and patted Randy on the shoulders.

"Randy, man, we're live," he said. "We got fifty people just watching the demo screens. Get that intro going, dude."

Jay waded through a mess of wires to get to the refrigerator and grab a beer, then resumed his post at the laptop monitoring the stream.

"Fuck, we got eighty now! Come on, dude, let's get this going."

Randy looked up at Blake and shrugged.

"I really didn't think of anything to say for an intro," he said.

"Well, just talk about yourself or something. How long you've been collecting. Things like that."

"I don't really wanna talk about myself. I'm not that interesting."

"You are interesting, dude," she said. "Come on. This is supposed to be a celebration. Of your hobby! 80 people clicked on the stream and we haven't really started yet. I mean, hell, we didn't even advertise this at all. We just put it out on Twitter and that's it."

"No, I know," said Randy. "And I really appreciate it. I really do. You guys have been amazing. It's just that I'm drawing a total fucking blank."

"Up to 100!" yelled Jay from across the room.

Blake smiled and, in a barely audible whisper made comprehensible only by reading the movement of her lips, she said "Do it for me."

"Ok. Fine." said Randy.

Blake refocused the camera and counted down from five, pointing at Randy to indicate that they were recording. Randy cleared his throat and began speaking, but his words were accompanied by the taste of blood, which began to pool between his cheeks. He tried to choke it back with a coarse grunt, but then felt a powerful wave of nausea, causing him to sink to the floor. His stomach and chest were beginning to convulse uncontrollably, and he could feel his legs going limp. Bracing himself on a stool, he struggled to his feet and ran out of the garage with a wobbling, uncoordinated stride.

He tripped on the cracked pavement of the driveway as he made his way to the house and into the kitchen, where he collapsed forward onto the sink and began to vomit. What little food he had in his system came up in soft pink chunks mixed with mucous, the sight of which induced more vomiting. He turned on the faucet to rinse away the evidence of his illness and wash the putrid taste out of his mouth. Still feeling lightheaded and weak, he sat down on the floor, rested his head against a windowsill on the wall behind him, and took deep breaths to calm himself.

Blake rushed in and, seeing a trail of small blood droplets on the floor and Randy struggling for air, began to panic.

"Oh fuck!" she screamed, "What's wrong?!"

Randy could only shake his head and hold up his hand in an attempt to dismiss her fears, while engaging in his usual breathing exercises to repress any further need to vomit. Blake knelt down beside him and caressed his face.

"What's wrong?" she whispered, "Please talk to me."

"Nothing," said Randy, forcing his voice through the film of mucous and vomit that remained in his throat. "Can you just get me my pills and some water?"

Blake stood up and started a frantic search of the kitchen.

"On the table," said Randy.

She located his bottle of Ativan under mound of papers, plastic bags, and empty food containers and handed it to him.

"I just need some water," he said, his voice crackling and breaking a part.

"I don't see any bottles."

"Just from the sink. I just need water."

"No, you can't drink that stuff" she said "I think we've got some water in the car."

"Please," he said, looking at her with an imploring weariness, "it doesn't matter. I just need a little water."

She stared at him for a few seconds, then shook her head in agreement and filled a glass, which he used to flush down two tablets.

"Please tell me what's going on," she said, sitting back down on the floor next to him and taking his hand.

"It's nothing," said Randy, "I just get these panic attacks. It's been happening a lot lately."

"Panic attacks? It looked like you couldn't breathe," she said.

"They're pretty bad" said Randy, "But they pass. These pills help."

"You want us to call an ambulance?"

"No, no, it's fine," he said, gripping the windowsill above him as he struggled to stand, "Once these pills kick in I'll be better. Let's go back."

"Look, let's just forget about this whole thing. Jay and I will just stay with you and we'll just chill," she said, still holding his hand and looking up at him.

"No, seriously. Let's do this. We're not wasting all of the work you guys put into this because of my stupid fucking panic attacks. Come on, I'm serious"

Blake stood up and pulled him closer to her. "Are you sure?"

"Yeah."

They walked to the door. Randy braced himself on the countertop and the chairs as he moved, still drawing deep breaths in an effort to regain his composure. He could feel the medication begin to take effect, with his pulse normalizing and the muscles of his chest and stomach relaxing.

Before stepping out onto the back stoop, he paused in the doorway and turned to Blake.

"I'm sorry," he said, cupping her face in his hands and kissing her on the forehead, allowing his lips to rest there for a few seconds, hoping to communicate in a gesture what he could not put into words.

She looked up at him, her eyes overcome with the piercing vulnerability she tried so hard to repress.

"Why?"

He walked back into the game room. Jay had begun to play a few of the consoles, jumping from one to the other in an attempt to keep the stream going in their absence.

"Dude, what the fuck happened?" asked Jay.

"Guess I drank too much," said Randy

Randy sat back on the stool in front of his shelves and tried to focus himself through more deep breathing. Blake hesitantly stood behind the camera, checked her settings, and made some minor adjustments to the lighting. Randy picked up the lavalier mic from the floor and reattached it to his T-shirt, clearing his throat and giving Blake a thumbs up.

"You know what you want to say?" she asked, making penetrating, unbreakable eye contact with him.

"Kind of," he said, "Let's just give it a go."

"You guys ok now?" shouted Jay.

"We're good," said Randy.

"Feed's ready. You're on," said Jay

Randy cleared his throat, but again felt a sense of panic as he stared into the red record light of the camera pointed at him. He steadied himself on the stool and looked at Blake, who stared back at him with loving, insistent attention. He decided to speak only to her.

"Well, uh, thanks for clicking onto this stream. I, uh, know we had some technical difficulties, but, uh, I think we're back and good to go. Ummm, I guess you can see the idea is to give you guys a sample of the various systems I've got here in my game room. Kind of like a little tour of the history of video games. You know, there used to be a time when this was a pretty common thing. Like, about 15 years ago or so. I'm not sure a lot of people care about this stuff anymore, but, um, I guess if you're watching this, you care. So, thanks.

I'm not going to talk about all the different games or systems right now. That stuff is in the different feeds and the description if you're interested. I'm just gonna talk about me. Why I got into gaming. I've been thinking a lot about it and, uh, I guess I don't really have a thrilling answer. I don't know where you guys are in the world, but we're coming to you from Wilkes-Barre, Pennsylvania tonight. It's a fucked up, dying city in the U.S. And honestly, some really sad and fucked up shit has happened to me over the past few weeks. I've been questioning a lot of things and I've actually been kicking myself for spending my life here in my game room and missing out on a lot of what life had to offer me. Even though, around here, it didn't offer much, I still felt guilty about just sitting here and doing nothing.

And so I asked myself. Why did I do it? What made me dedicate myself to this hobby? Why did I need all of this stuff? And I didn't really have an answer until tonight. And it's a simple answer. Maybe you guys'll think it's a stupid answer. And here it is: I collected this stuff not because I'm an obsessive-compulsive maniac or because I'm some man-child. I did it because video games are fun. Plain and simple.

Sounds dumb, right? But, uh, think about it from my perspective. I was born before a lot of people had the Internet. I grew up just about the time when this country went to shit. And you know what, video games were just fucking fun. When I was a kid, if I was lucky, I could drag my SNES into my room and lose myself for hours in Hyrule. I had to walk to Blockbuster to rent my PS2 games. I had to stand in lines to buy new releases. I had to do all this shit in the world and, for a few hours, I could escape into the digital worlds of video games. And they were so much cooler than what was on TV or in the movies. They were so much more interesting than what was in the papers and in the news.

Um, let's see. As, uh, as time went on, that experience of escapism and immersion spread beyond video games. And then before you knew it, everything was starting to become a digital world in one way or another. And, for me anyway, it stopped being fun. Getting achievements on Xbox Live was cool at first, but now I get achievement notifications if I work so many hours at my shit job. I mean, fuck, my dentist once told me to sync my toothbrush to my smartphone and compete in some oral hygiene competition. Not exactly what I had in mind when I played *Phantasy Star Online* and dreamed about the future.

So yeah, the more the digitized version of the 'real world' became a drag, the more I went back to old games. I collected stuff from as way back as the 70s. A lot of the time I didn't even have a nostalgic connection to what I was buying. I was just addicted to the thrill of the hunt and to imagining the days when you played a game, escaped for a bit, and returned to a real world that wasn't a parasitic fucking shithole. I guess I just loved that illusion—I loved deceiving myself into believing that the world I would return to after a gaming session was the one I remembered from my childhood. Not sure if that makes sense to you guys, but it's just how I feel at the moment.

209

And of course the ironic part is that, the more I collected to capture that feeling, the more I sank into my own little world here, and squandered whatever chance I had at finding meaningful moments outside of gaming. But recently, lots of shit has kind of forced me to re-engage with my life. And a lot of it has really sucked, but I've lived through some amazing moments that I'll never forget.

So yeah, that's my message, I guess. Play old games. Remember a time when games offered us a chance to escape for a bit without asking for credit cards, finger prints, GPS data, and retinal scans. Remember a time when games existed just to be fun. Appreciate the ability to save, power off, and return to whatever good stuff is left in the real world. It's harder today. The real world is fucked up. But if you can find someone or something that gives your life meaning, chase it."

The red light of the camera went off and Randy took a deep breath. Though he was unsure if he had said too much that would give away his relationship with Blake, he felt relieved by having communicated, however incompletely, what their relationship had meant to him. He looked over at Jay, wondering whether he had picked up on the subtext of his speech, but Jay was engrossed in managing the stream and did not give any indication that he had paid attention to Randy's introduction.

"That was awesome," said Blake, sniffling as she watched some of the footage back on the camera. "It doesn't matter who watches this, what you said meant something, even if only to you and me. That's what's important."

"Fuck," said Jay, "we're up to 120 people. This is awesome. We're listed in the top twenty streams!"

"Nice," said Randy, "you up for some Virtua Fighter?"

"You're on," said Jay.

Randy and Jay played several friendly rounds of *Virtua Fighter 2* on the arcade cabinet, while Blake and Jay's colleague from work started playing Atari 2600 and Colecovision and, after a ten-minute interval, switched off to the next two systems on the console timeline. Eventually, Blake's college friends, a couple, arrived and joined the stream, gravitating to the Nintendo Wii before discovering the Virtua Boy and the Vectrex, which they played with amused curiosity. Randy and Jay glanced back at the streaming stats from time to time and saw that the viewer count was steadily climbing and that a lively chat had started, with viewers writing about their gaming memories in quick succession.

After fighting Jay to a draw in ten matches of *Virtua Fighter*, Randy stepped back and just observed the game room with a sense of contentment and appreciation. His gathering was pathetic when compared with the arcade party at Big Jeff's, but there was something more authentic about this game night. His collection didn't consist of trophies to be locked away in a vault, but of real objects, generating real pleasure. The collection wasn't merely an extravagant prop used as an excuse to throw a posh party, but a testament to the power of games to bring people together in the spirit of fun.

Blake was now sitting on the couch, playing *Bonk's Adventure* on the Turbo Duo for the first time. She snickered as Bonk snacked on the meat power-ups and, in a whirl of smiley faces and mushroom clouds, transformed himself into a demonic, invincible caveman. It seemed amazing to Randy that a game from 1989 could still elicit such an innocent, playful reaction in 2030. Even more astounding was that over a thousand viewers were watching them play and were rediscovering games from the past. The cynicism and self-doubt with which he viewed the idea of the game night seemed silly in retrospect, and he was grateful that Blake and Jay insisted that he go through with it.

Randy sat down at the card table with a beer to read more comments. The viewer count kept ticking upward and the chat box was flooded with warm recollections and expressions of gratitude to Randy for hosting the game night. As he scrolled down the screen to keep up with the furiously expanding chat activity, a pale, red light filled the room. At first, it came through the back window near his computer desk and then, following a violent rush of air, shined through the garage door windows, oscillating from one side of the room to the other. Someone violently kicked in the rear garage door, and a group of men with assault rifles stormed into the game room, all dressed in black bullet-proof vests, black pants, and ski masks.

"Hands up now!" barked one of the men, pointing a rifle at Randy, as one of his colleagues walked behind him and threw open the rest of the garage doors.

More armed men were positioned outside in the driveway, and behind them a group of armored vans and police cars. The drone flew overhead, using its thrusters to hover behind the officers and point its weapons array at the entrance to the garage, its red scanner light flickering.

An unmasked man stepped through the crowd of officers and into the game room. He was wearing a black SWAT team uniform, but no police badges or other identifying insignias were visible on his vest. He laughed and raised his left hand—a signal to the other officers to lower their rifles.

"Hell of a stream," he said, surveying the room. "So entertaining, I'm kinda sorry to break it up. Now, which one of you is Mr. Randy James"

Randy, Blake, and Jay stared at each other with blank nervousness, until eventually Randy stepped forward.

"I am. Is there a problem, officer?"

The man walked over to Randy and extended his hand.

"Nice to meet you, Randy, I'm Sargent Evans," he said.

They shook hands. The Sargent then turned around and nodded to one of his men, who walked over and jabbed Randy in the chest with the butt of his rifle. The blow was vicious and precise, landing right on the part of his sternum under which his tumor grew, causing Randy to fall to his knees and clutch his chest in pain.

"Now the problem with this stream," the Sargent continued, "is that your showing footage from hardware that, according to my knowledge, has never been registered with any government authority. In fact, our data indicate that you have storage devices in here with illegally obtained digital content amassed over a twenty-year period. Software theft is a serious crime, Mr. James, and I doubt you have the funds to pay restitution to the companies you stole this stuff from."

He walked over and inspected the arcade cabinet.

"Ramirez," he yelled, "open this up and remove the device inside. Try to determine how many copyright infringements exist on the hard drive. Jackson, grab the computer in the back and check for the same. Antero, I need you to confiscate all of the hardware on that shelf. Some of it might be stolen."

The Sargent then walked over to Randy, who was still quivering in pain from the blow to his chest, and put his hand on Randy's shoulder.

"I know that young people feel that they're untouchable but, at your age, I'd a thought you'd get rid of this contraband. Not smart, my friend. Not smart. Now get up."

Randy pulled his head off of the floor and wiped the blood from his mouth. He tried to stand, but his legs felt like jelly, causing him to fall back down and remain kneeling.

"Mr. James, I need you to make a statement," said the Sargent, turning away from him. "It'll be off the record, but it could help you in the long run. Now, answer honestly. How did you obtain all of these illegal devices?"

Randy again tried to straighten his body in an attempt to speak through the pain and offer a response. Everything then went black. A rope tightened around his neck and his face was slammed into the ground, crushing his glasses. His hands were forced behind his back and his wrists were bound together with high-pitched clicks of plastic. He struggled. Faint screams were audible. A blow to his liver made his body go numb. His ankles were tied. He felt pressure under his arms. His body seemed to float. Warm air turned cold. He hit a sheet of metal, face down. Tears rolled down his cheeks and pooled at the taut fabric under his chin. A door slammed behind him.

41927591R10129

Printed in Poland
by Amazon Fulfillment
Poland Sp. z o.o., Wrocław